So you think you already know about
The Princess Diaries?

*I*n your hands you are holding the story of Mia
Thermopolis. Sure, you may think you already
know it. The thing is, you don't. The fact is, books are
usually different from the movie versions, and *The
Princess Diaries* is no exception. Movies are good and
everything, but sometimes, to get the full story, you
have to go back to where it all began.

So, to help you discover the *real* Princess Mia, we are
giving you this free copy of *The Princess Diaries*, the first in
the series of books the movies were based on. We are sure
that once you start reading about Mia, you won't be able
to stop, so be sure to look in the back of this free book for
a list of all the titles in this amazing series, along with lots
of other books by Meg Cabot.

Now, get ready to enter the diary of Mia
Thermopolis!

MEG CABOT

THE *Princess* DIARIES

HarperTrophy®
An Imprint of HarperCollins Publishers

HarperTrophy® is a registered trademark of
HarperCollins Publishers.

The Princess Diaries
Copyright © 2000 by Meggin Cabot

Library of Congress Cataloging-in-Publication Data
Cabot, Meg.
    The princess diaries / Meg Cabot.
        p.   cm.
    Summary: Fourteen-year-old Mia, who is trying to lead a normal
life as a teenage girl in New York City, is shocked to learn that her
father is the Prince of Genovia, a small European principality, and
that she is a princess and the heir to the throne.
    ISBN-10: 0-06-114191-7 — ISBN-13: 978-0-06-114191-1
    [1. Princesses—Fiction.   2. Fathers and daughters—Fiction.
3. Identity—Fiction.   4. Diaries—Fiction.   5. New York City
(N.Y.)—Fiction.]
I. Title.
PZ7.C11165 Pr   2000   99-46479
[Fic]—dc21

❖

ACKNOWLEDGMENTS

The author wishes to express her gratitude to the people who contributed in so many ways to the creation and publication of this book: Beth Ader, Jennifer Brown, Barbara Cabot, Charles and Bonnie Egnatz, Emily Faith, Laura Langlie, Ron Markman, Abigail McAden, A. Elizabeth Mikesell, Melinda Mounsey, David Walton, Allegra Yeley and, most especially, Benjamin Egnatz.

"Whatever comes," she said,
"cannot alter one thing.
If I am a princess in rags and tatters,
I can be a princess inside.
It would be easy to be a princess if I were
dressed in cloth of gold, but it is a great
deal more of a triumph to be one all the
time when no one knows it."

A LITTLE PRINCESS
Frances Hodgson Burnett

Sometimes it seems like all I ever do is lie.

My mom thinks I'm repressing my feelings about this. I say to her, "No, Mom, I'm not. I think it's really neat. As long as you're happy, I'm happy."

Mom says, "I don't think you're being honest with me."

Then she hands me this book. She tells me she wants me to write down my feelings in this book, since, she says, I obviously don't feel I can talk about them with her.

She wants me to write down my feelings? Okay, I'll write down my feelings:

I CAN'T BELIEVE SHE'S DOING THIS TO ME!

Like everybody doesn't *already* think I'm a freak. I'm practically the biggest freak in the entire school. I mean, let's face it: I'm five foot nine, flat-chested, and a freshman. How much *more* of a freak could I be?

If people at school find out about this, I'm dead. That's it. Dead.

Oh, God, if you really do exist, please don't let them find out about this.

There are four million people in Manhattan, right? That makes about two million of them guys. So out of TWO MILLION guys, she has to go out with Mr. Gianini. She can't go out with some guy I don't know.

She can't go out with some guy she met at D'Agostinos or wherever. Oh, no.

She has to go out with my Algebra teacher.

Thanks, Mom. Thanks a whole lot.

Lilly's like, "Mr. Gianini's cool."

Yeah, right. He's cool if you're Lilly Moscovitz. He's cool if you're good at Algebra, like Lilly Moscovitz. He's not so cool if you're flunking Algebra, like me.

He's not so cool if he makes you stay after school EVERY SINGLE SOLITARY DAY from 2:30 to 3:30 to practice the FOIL method when you could be hanging out with all your friends. He's not so cool if he calls your mother in for a parent/teacher conference to talk about how you're flunking Algebra, then ASKS HER OUT.

And he's not so cool if he's sticking his tongue in your mom's mouth.

Not that I've actually seen them do this. They haven't even been on their first date yet. And I don't think my mom would let a guy put his tongue in her mouth on the first date.

At least, I hope not.

I saw Josh Richter stick his tongue in Lana Weinberger's mouth last week. I had this totally close-up view of it, since they were leaning up against Josh's locker, which is right next to mine. It kind of grossed me out.

Though I can't say I'd mind if Josh Richter kissed *me* like that. The other day Lilly and I were at Bigelows picking up some alpha hydroxy for Lilly's mom, and I noticed Josh waiting at the checkout counter. He saw me and he actually sort of smiled and said, "Hey."

He was buying Drakkar Noir, a men's cologne. I got a free sample of it from the salesgirl. Now I can smell Josh whenever I want to, in the privacy of my own home.

Lilly says Josh's synapses were probably misfiring that day, due to heatstroke or something. She said he probably thought I looked familiar but couldn't place my face without the cement block walls of Albert Einstein High behind me. Why else, she asked, would the most popular senior in high school say hey to me, Mia Thermopolis, a lowly freshman?

But I know it wasn't heatstroke. The truth is, when he's away from Lana and all his jock friends, Josh is a totally different person. The kind of person who doesn't care if a girl is flat-chested or wears size-ten shoes. The kind of person who can see beyond all that into the depths of a girl's soul. I know because when I looked into his eyes that day at Bigelows, I saw the deeply sensitive person inside him, struggling to get out.

Lilly says I have an overactive imagination and a pathological need to invent drama in my life. She says the fact that I'm so upset about my mom and Mr. G is a classic example.

"If you're that upset about it, just *tell* your mom," Lilly says. "*Tell* her you don't want her going out with him. I don't understand you, Mia. You're always going around, lying about how you feel. Why don't you just assert yourself for a change? Your feelings have worth, you know."

Oh, right. Like I'm going to bum my mom out like that. She's so totally happy about this date, it's enough to make me want to throw up. She goes around *cooking* all the time. I'm not even kidding. She made pasta for the first time last night in like months. I had already opened the Suzie's Chinese take-out menu, and she says, "Oh, no cold sesame noodles tonight, honey. I made pasta."

Pasta! My mom made *pasta*!

She even observed my rights as a vegetarian and didn't put any meatballs in the sauce.

I don't understand any of this.

THINGS TO DO

1. Buy cat litter
2. Finish FOIL worksheet for Mr. G
3. Stop telling Lilly everything
4. Go to Pearl Paint: get soft lead pencils, spray mount, canvas stretchers (for Mom)
5. World Civ report on Iceland (5 pages, double space)
6. Stop thinking so much about Josh Richter
7. Drop off laundry
8. October rent (make sure Mom has deposited Dad's check!!!)
9. Be more assertive
10. Measure chest

In Algebra today all I could think about was how Mr. Gianini might put his tongue in my mom's mouth tomorrow night during their date. I just sat there, staring at him. He asked me a really easy question—I swear, he saves all the easy ones for me, like he doesn't want me to feel left out or something—and I totally didn't even hear it. I was like, "What?"

Then Lana Weinberger made that sound she always makes and leaned over to me so that all her blond hair swished onto my desk. I got hit by this giant wave of perfume, and then Lana hissed in this really mean voice:

"FREAK."

Only she said it like it had more than one syllable. Like it was spelled FUR-REEK.

How come nice people like Princess Diana get killed in car wrecks but mean people like Lana never do? I don't understand what Josh Richter sees in her. I mean, yeah, she's pretty. But she's so *mean*. Doesn't he *notice*?

Maybe Lana is nice to Josh, though. *I'd* sure be nice to Josh. He is the best-looking boy in Albert Einstein High School. A lot of the boys look totally geeky in our school's uniform, which for boys is gray pants, white shirt, and black sweater, long-sleeved or vest. Not Josh, though. He looks like a model in his uniform. I am not kidding.

Anyway. Today I noticed that Mr. Gianini's nostrils stick out A LOT. Why would you want to go out with a guy whose nostrils stick out so much? I asked Lilly this at lunch and she said, "I've never noticed his nostrils before. Are you gonna eat that dumpling?"

Lilly says I need to stop obsessing. She says I'm taking my anxiety over the fact that this is only our first month in high school and I already have an F in something, and transferring it to anxiety about Mr. Gianini and my mom. She says this is called displacement.

It sort of sucks when your best friend's parents are psychoanalysts.

Today after school the Drs. Moscovitz were totally trying to analyze me. I mean, Lilly and I were just sitting there playing Boggle. And every five minutes it was like, "Girls, do you want some Snapple? Girls, there's a very interesting squid documentary on the Discovery channel. And by the way, Mia, how do you feel about your mother starting to date your Algebra teacher?"

I said, "I feel fine about it."

Why can't I be more assertive?

But what if Lilly's parents run into my mom at Jefferson Market or something? If I told them the truth, they'd *definitely* tell her. I don't want my mom to know how weird I feel about this, not when she's so happy about it.

The worst part was that Lilly's older brother Michael overheard the whole thing. He immediately started laughing his head off, even though I don't see anything funny about it.

He went, "*Your* mom is dating Frank Gianini? Ha! Ha! Ha!"

So great. Now Lilly's brother Michael knows.

So then I had to start begging him not to tell anybody. He's in fifth period Gifted and Talented class with me and Lilly, which is the biggest joke of a class, because Mrs. Hill, who's in charge of the G and T program at Albert Einstein, doesn't care what we do as long as we don't make too much noise. She hates it when she has to come out of the teachers' lounge, which is right across the hall from the G and T room, to yell at us.

Anyway, Michael is supposed to use fifth period to work on his on-line webzine, *Crackhead*. I'm supposed to use it for catching up on my Algebra homework.

But anyway, Mrs. Hill never checks to see what we're doing in G and T, which is probably good, since mostly what we're all doing is figuring out ways to lock the new Russian kid, who's supposedly this musical genius, in the supply closet so we don't have to listen to any more Stravinsky on his stupid violin.

But don't think that just because Michael and I are united against Boris Pelkowski and his violin he'd keep quiet about my mom and Mr. G.

What Michael kept saying was, "What'll you do for me, huh, Thermopolis? What'll you do for me?"

But there's nothing I can do for Michael Moscovitz.

I can't offer to do his homework, or anything. Michael is a senior (just like Josh Richter). Michael has gotten all straight A's his entire life (just like Josh Richter). Michael will probably go to Yale or Harvard next year (just like Josh Richter).

What could *I* do for someone like that?

Not that Michael's perfect, or anything. Unlike Josh Richter, Michael is not on the crew team. Michael isn't even on the debate team. Michael does not believe in organized sports, or organized religion, or organized anything, for that matter. Instead, Michael spends almost all of his time in his room. I once asked Lilly what he does in there, and she said she and her parents employ a don't ask, don't tell policy with Michael.

I bet he's in there making a bomb. Maybe he'll blow up Albert Einstein High School as a senior prank.

Occasionally, Michael comes out of his room and makes sarcastic comments. Sometimes when he does this he is not wearing a shirt. Even though he does not believe in organized sports, I have noticed that Michael has a really nice chest. His stomach muscles are extremely well defined.

I have never mentioned this to Lilly.

Anyway, I guess Michael got tired of my offering to do stuff like walk his sheltie, Pavlov, and take his mom's empty Tab cans back to Gristedes for the deposit money, which is his weekly chore. Because in the end Michael just said, in this disgusted voice, "Forget it, okay, Thermopolis?" and went back into his room.

I asked Lilly why he was so mad, and she said because he'd been sexually harassing me but I didn't notice.

How embarrassing! Supposing Josh Richter starts sexually harassing me someday (I wish) and I don't notice? God, I'm so stupid sometimes.

Anyway, Lilly said not to worry about Michael telling his friends at school about my mom and Mr. G, since Michael has no friends. Then Lilly wanted to know why I cared about Mr. Gianini's nostrils sticking out so much, since I'm not the one who has to look at them, my mom is.

And I said, "Excuse me, I have to look at them from 9:55 to 10:55 and from 2:30 to 3:30 EVERY SINGLE DAY, except Saturdays and Sundays and national holidays and the summer. If I don't flunk, that is, and have to go to summer school."

And if they get married, then I'll have to look at them EVERY SINGLE DAY, SEVEN DAYS A WEEK, MAJOR HOLIDAYS INCLUDED.

Define set: collection of objects; element or member belongs to a set

A = {Gilligan, Skipper, Mary Ann}
rule specifies each element
A = {x|x is one of the castaways on *Gilligan's Island*}

LILLY MOSCOVITZ'S LIST OF
HOTTEST GUYS

(compiled during World Civ, with commentary
by Mia Thermopolis)

1. *Josh Richter* (agree—six feet of unadulterated hotness. Blond hair, often falling into his clear blue eyes, and that sweet, sleepy smile. Only drawback: he has the bad taste to date Lana Weinberger)

2. *Boris Pelkowski* (strongly disagree. Just because he played his stupid violin at Carnegie Hall when he was twelve does not make him hot. Plus he tucks his school sweater into his pants, instead of wearing it out, like a normal person)

3. *Pierce Brosnan, best James Bond ever* (disagree—I liked Timothy Dalton better)

4. *Daniel Day Lewis in* Last of the Mohicans (agree—stay alive, no matter what occurs)

5. *Prince William of England* (duh)

6. *Leonardo in* Titanic (As if! That is so 1998)

7. *Mr. Wheeton, the crew coach* (hot, but taken. Seen opening the door to the teachers' lounge for Mademoiselle Klein)

8. *That guy in that jeans ad on that giant billboard in Times Square* (totally agree. Who IS that guy? They should give him his own TV series)

9. *Dr. Quinn Medicine Woman's boyfriend* (whatever happened to him? He was hot!)
10. *Joshua Bell, the violinist* (totally agree. It would be so cool to date a musician—just not Boris Pelkowski)

I was measuring my chest and totally not thinking about the fact that my mom was out with my Algebra teacher when my dad called. I don't know why, but I lied and told him Mom was at her studio. Which is so weird, because obviously Dad knows Mom dates. But for some reason, I just couldn't tell him about Mr. Gianini.

This afternoon during my mandatory review session with Mr. Gianini, I was sitting there practicing the FOIL method (first, outside, inside, last; first, outside, inside, last—Oh my God, when am I ever going to have to actually use the FOIL method in real life? WHEN???) and all of a sudden Mr. Gianini said, "Mia, I hope you don't feel, well, uncomfortable about my seeing your mother socially."

Only for some reason for a second I thought he said SEXUALLY, not socially. And then I could feel my face getting totally hot. I mean like BURNING. And I said, "Oh, no, Mr. Gianini, it doesn't bother me at all."

And Mr. Gianini said, "Because if it bothers you, we can talk about it."

I guess he must have figured out I was lying, since my face was so red.

But all I said was, "Really, it doesn't bother me. I mean, it bothers me a LITTLE, but really, I'm fine with it. I mean, it's just a date, right? Why get upset about one measly date?"

That was when Mr. Gianini said, "Well, Mia, I don't know if it's going to be one measly date. I really like your mother."

And then, I don't even know how, but all of a sudden I heard myself saying, "Well, you better. Because if you do anything to make her cry, I'll kick your butt."

Oh my God! I can't even believe I said the word *butt* to a teacher! My face got even REDDER after that, which I wouldn't have thought possible. Why is it that the only time I can tell the truth is when it's guaranteed to get me into trouble?

But I guess I *am* feeling sort of weird about the whole thing. Maybe Lilly's parents were right.

Mr. Gianini, though, was totally cool. He smiled in this funny way and said, "I have no intention of making your mother cry, but if I ever do, you have my permission to kick my butt."

So that was okay, sort of.

Anyway, Dad sounded really weird on the phone. But then again, he always does. Transatlantic phone calls suck because I can hear the ocean swishing around in the background and it makes me all nervous, like the fish are listening, or something. Plus Dad didn't even want to talk to me. He wanted to talk to Mom. I suppose somebody died, and he wants Mom to break it to me gently.

Maybe it was Grandmère. Hmmm. . . .

My breasts have grown exactly *none* since last

summer. Mom was totally wrong. I did *not* have a growth spurt when I turned fourteen, like she did. I will probably *never* have a growth spurt, at least not on my chest. I only have growth spurts UP, not OUT. I am now the tallest girl in my class.

Now if anybody asks me to the Cultural Diversity Dance next month (yeah, right) I won't be able to wear a strapless dress because there isn't anything on my chest to hold it up.

Saturday, September 27

I was asleep when my mom got home from her date last night (I stayed up as late as I could, because I wanted to know what happened, but I guess all that measuring wore me out), so I didn't get to ask her how it went until this morning when I went out into the kitchen to feed Fat Louie. Mom was up already, which was weird, because usually she sleeps later than me, and *I'm* a teenager, *I'm* supposed to be the one sleeping all the time.

But Mom's been depressed ever since her last boyfriend turned out to be a Republican.

Anyway, she was in there, humming in a happy way and making pancakes. I nearly died of shock to see her actually cooking something so early in the morning, let alone something vegetarian.

Of course she had a fabulous time. They went to dinner at Monte's (not too shabby, Mr. G!) and then walked around the West Village and went to some bar and sat outside in the back garden until nearly two in the morning, just talking. I kind of tried to find out if there'd been any kissing, particularly of the tongue-in-mouth variety, but my mom just smiled and looked all embarrassed.

Okay. Gross.

They're going out again this week.

I guess I don't mind, if it makes her this happy.

Today Lilly is shooting a spoof of the movie *The Blair Witch Project* for her TV show, *Lilly Tells It Like It Is*. *The Blair Witch Project* is about some kids who go out into the woods to find a witch and end up disappearing. All that's found of them is film footage and some piles of sticks. Only instead of *The Blair Witch Project*, Lilly's version is called *The Green Witch Project*. Lilly intends to take a handheld camera down to Washington Square Park and film the tourists who come up to us and ask if we know how to get to Green Witch Village. (It's actually Greenwich Village—you're not supposed to pronounce the *w* in *Greenwich*. But people from out of town always say it wrong.)

Anyway, as tourists come up and ask us which way to Green Witch Village, we are supposed to start screaming and run away in terror. All that will be left of us by the end, Lilly says, is a little pile of MetroCards. Lilly says after the show is aired no one will ever think of MetroCards the same way.

I said it was too bad we don't have a real witch. I thought we could get Lana Weinberger to play her, but Lilly said that would be typecasting. Plus then we'd have to put up with Lana all day, and nobody would want that. Like she'd even show up, considering how she thinks we're the most unpopular girls in the whole school. She probably wouldn't want to tarnish her reputation by being seen with us.

Then again, she's so vain she'd probably jump at the

chance to be on TV, even if it *is* only a public access channel.

After filming was over for the day, we all saw the Blind Guy crossing Bleecker. He had a new victim, this totally innocent German tourist who had no idea that the nice blind man she was helping to cross the street was going to feel her up as soon as they got to the other side, then pretend he hadn't done it on purpose.

Just my luck, the only guy who's ever felt me up (not that there's anything to feel) was BLIND.

Lilly says she's going to report the Blind Guy to the Sixth Precinct. Like they would care. They've got more important things to worry about. Like catching murderers.

THINGS TO DO

1. Get cat litter
2. Make sure Mom sent out rent check
3. Stop lying
4. Proposal for English paper
5. Pick up laundry
6. Stop thinking about Josh Richter

My dad called again today, and this time Mom really *was* at her studio, so I didn't feel so bad about lying last night and not telling him about Mr. Gianini. He sounded all weird on the phone again, so finally I was like, "Dad, is Grandmère dead?" and he got all startled and said, "No, Mia, why would you think that?"

And I told him it was because he sounded so weird, and he was all, "I don't sound weird," which was a lie, because he DID sound weird. But I decided to let it drop, and I talked to him about Iceland, because we're studying Iceland in World Civ. Iceland has the world's highest literacy rate, because there's nothing to do there but read. They also have these natural hot springs, and everybody goes swimming in them. Once, the opera came to Iceland, and every show was sold out and something like 98 percent of the population attended. Everybody knew all the words to the opera and went around singing it all day.

I would like to live in Iceland someday. It sounds like a fun place. Much more fun than Manhattan, where people sometimes spit at you for no reason.

But Dad didn't seem all that impressed by Iceland. I suppose by comparison, Iceland does make every other country look sucky. The country Dad lives in is pretty small, though. I would think if the opera went there, about 80 percent of the population would attend, which would certainly be something to be proud of.

I only shared this information with him because he is a politician, and I thought it might give him some ideas about how to make things better in Genovia, where he lives. But I guess Genovia doesn't need to be better. Genovia's number one import is tourists. I know this because I had to do a fact sheet on every country in Europe in the seventh grade, and Genovia was right up there with Disneyland as far as income from the tourist trade is concerned. That's probably why people in Genovia don't have to pay taxes: The government already has enough money. This is called a principality. The only other one is Monaco. My dad says we have a lot of cousins in Monaco, but so far I haven't met any of them, not even at Grandmère's.

I suggested to Dad that next summer, instead of spending it with him and Grandmère at her French chateau, Miragnac, we go to Iceland. We'd have to leave my grandmother at the chateau, of course. She'd hate Iceland. She hates any place where you can't order up a decent Sidecar, which is her favorite drink, twenty-four hours a day.

All Dad said was, "We'll talk about that some other time," and hung up.

Mom is so right about him.

Absolute value: the distance that a given number is from zero on a number line . . . always a positive

Today I watched Mr. Gianini very closely for signs that he might not have had as good a time on his date with my mom as my mom did. He seemed to be in a really good mood, though. During class, while we were working on the quadratic formula (what happened to FOIL? I was just starting to get the hang of it, and all of a sudden there's some NEW thing; no *wonder* I'm flunking), he asked if anybody had gone out for a part in the fall musical, *My Fair Lady*.

Then later he said, in the way he does when he gets excited about something, "You know who would be a good Eliza Doolittle? Mia, I think you would."

I thought I would totally die. I know Mr. Gianini was only trying to be nice—I mean, he is dating my mom, after all—but he was SO far off: First of all because of course they already held auditions, and even if I could've gone out for a part (which I couldn't, because I'm flunking Algebra, hello, Mr. Gianini, remember?) I NEVER would've gotten one, let alone the LEAD. I can't sing. I can barely even *talk*.

Even Lana Weinberger, who always got the lead in junior high, didn't get the lead. It went to some senior girl. Lana plays a maid, a spectator at the Ascot Races, and a Cockney hooker. Lilly is house manager. Her job is to flick the lights on and off at the end of intermission.

I was so freaked out by what Mr. Gianini said I couldn't even *say* anything. I just sat there and felt myself turning all red. Maybe that was why later, when Lilly and I went by my locker at lunch, Lana, who was there waiting for Josh, was all, "Oh, hello, *Amelia*," in her snottiest voice, even though nobody has called me Amelia (except Grandmère) since kindergarten, when I asked everybody not to.

Then, as I bent over to get my money out of my backpack, Lana must have got a good look down my blouse, because all of a sudden she goes, "Oh, how sweet. I see we still can't fit into a bra. Might I suggest Band-Aids?"

I would have hauled off and slugged her—well, probably not; the Drs. Moscovitz say I have issues about confrontation—if Josh Richter hadn't walked up AT THAT VERY MOMENT. I knew he totally heard, but all he said was, "Can I get by here?" to Lilly, since she was blocking his path to his locker.

I was ready to go slinking down to the cafeteria and forget the whole thing—God, that's all I need, my lack of chest pointed out *right in front* of Josh Richter!—but Lilly couldn't leave well enough alone. She got all red in the face and said to Lana, "Why don't you do us all a favor and go curl up someplace and die, Weinberger?"

Well, nobody tells Lana Weinberger to go curl up someplace and die. I mean, nobody. Not if she doesn't want her name written up all over the walls of the girls' room. Not that this would be such a heinous thing—I mean, no boys are going to see it in the girls' room—but I sort of like keeping my name off walls, for the most part.

But Lilly doesn't care about things like that. I mean, she's short and sort of round and kind of resembles a pug, but she totally doesn't care how she looks. I mean, she has her own TV show, and guys call in all the time and say how ugly they think she is, and ask her to lift her shirt up (*she* isn't flat-chested; she wears a C cup already), and she just laughs and laughs.

Lilly isn't afraid of anything.

So when Lana Weinberger started in on her for telling her to curl up and die, Lilly just blinked up at her and was like, "Bite me."

The whole thing would have escalated into this giant girl fight—Lilly has seen every single episode of *Xena: Warrior Princess*, and can kickbox like nobody's business—if Josh Richter hadn't slammed his locker door closed and said "I'm outta here" in a disgusted voice. That was when Lana just dropped it like a hot potato and scooted after him, going, "Josh, wait up. Wait up, Josh!"

Lilly and I just stood there looking at each other like we couldn't believe it. I still can't. Who *are* these people, and why do I have to be incarcerated with them on a daily basis?

HOMEWORK

Algebra: problems 1–12, pg. 79
English: proposal
World Civ: questions at end of Chapter 4
G&T: none
French: use *avoir* in neg. sentence, rd. lessons one
to three, pas de plus
Biology: none

$B = \{x \mid x \text{ is an integer}\}$
$D = \{2,3,4\}$
4ED
5ED
$E = \{x \mid x \text{ is an integer greater than 4 but less than 258}\}$

Something really weird just happened. I got home from school, and my mom was there (she's usually at her studio all day during the week). She had this funny look on her face, and then she went, "I have to talk to you."

She wasn't humming anymore, and she hadn't cooked anything, so I knew it was serious.

I was kind of hoping Grandmère was dead, but I knew it had to be much worse than that, and I was worried something had happened to Fat Louie, like he'd swallowed another sock. The last time he did that, the vet charged us $1,000 to remove the sock from his small intestines, and he walked around with a funny look on his face for about a month.

Fat Louie, I mean. Not the vet.

But it turned out it wasn't about my cat, it was about my dad. The reason my dad kept on calling was because he wanted to tell us that he just found out, because of his cancer, that he can't have any more kids.

Cancer is a scary thing. Fortunately, the kind of cancer my dad had was pretty curable. They just had to cut off the cancerous part, and then he had to have chemo, and after a year, so far, the cancer hasn't come back.

Unfortunately, the part they had to cut off was . . .

Ew, I don't even like writing it.

His *testicle*.

GROSS!

It turns out that when they cut off one of your testicles, and then give you chemo, you have like a really strong chance of becoming sterile. Which is what my dad just found out he is.

Mom says he's really bummed out. She says we have to be very understanding of him right now, because men have needs, and one of them is the need to feel progenitively omnipotent.

What I don't get is, what's the big deal? What does he need more kids for? He already has me! Sure, I only see him summers and at Christmastime, but that's enough, right? I mean, he's pretty busy running Genovia. It's no joke trying to make a whole country, even one that's only a mile long, run smoothly. The only other things he has time for besides me are his girlfriends. He's always got some new girlfriend slinking around. He brings them with him when we go to Grandmère's place in France in the summer. They always drool all over the pools and the stables and the waterfall and the twenty-seven bedrooms and the ballroom and the vineyard and the farm and the airstrip.

And then he dumps them a week later.

I didn't know he wanted to *marry* one of them and have kids.

I mean, he never married my mom. My mom says that's because at the time she rejected the bourgeois mores of a society that didn't even accept women as equals to men and refused to recognize her rights as an individual.

I kind of always thought that maybe my dad just never asked her.

Anyway, my mom says Dad is flying here to New York tomorrow to talk to me about this. I don't know *why*. I mean, it doesn't have anything to do with *me*. But when I said to my mom, "Why does Dad have to fly all the way over here to talk to me about how he can't have kids?" she got this funny look on her face and started to say something, and then she stopped.

Then she just said, "You'll have to ask your father."

This is bad. My mom only says "Ask your father" when I want to know something she doesn't feel like telling me, like why people sometimes kill their own babies and how come Americans eat so much red meat and read so much less than the people of Iceland.

Note to self: Look up the words *progenitive, omnipotent,* and *mores*

distributive law
$5x + 5y - 5$
$5(x + y - 1)$

Distribute WHAT??? FIND OUT BEFORE QUIZ!!!

My dad's here. Well, not here in the loft. He's staying at the Plaza, as usual. I'm supposed to go see him tomorrow, after he's "rested." My dad rests a lot, now that he's had cancer. He stopped playing polo, too. But I think that's because one time a horse stepped on him.

Anyway, I hate the Plaza. Last time my dad stayed there, they wouldn't let me in to see him because I was wearing shorts. The lady who owns the place was there, they said, and she doesn't like to see people in cutoffs in the lobby of her fancy hotel. I had to call my dad from a house phone and ask him to bring down a pair of pants. He just told me to put the concierge on the phone, and the next thing you know, everybody was apologizing to me like crazy. They gave me this big basket filled with fruit and chocolate. It was cool. I didn't want the fruit, though, so I gave it to a homeless man I saw on the subway on my way back down to the Village. I don't think the homeless man wanted the fruit either, since he threw it all in the gutter and just kept the basket to use as a hat.

I told Lilly about what my dad said, about not being able to have kids, and she said that was very telling. She said it revealed that my dad still has unresolved issues with his parents, and I said, "Well, duh. Grandmère is a *huge* pain in the ass."

Lilly said she couldn't comment on the veracity of

that statement since she'd never met my grandmother. I've been asking if I could invite Lilly to Miragnac for like years, but Grandmère always says no. She says young people give her migraines.

Lilly says maybe my dad is afraid of losing his youth, which many men equate with losing their virility. I really think they should move Lilly up a grade, but she says she likes being a freshman. She says this way she has four whole years to make observations on the adolescent condition in post–Cold War America.

STARTING TODAY I WILL

1. Be nice to everyone, whether I like him/her or not
2. Stop lying all the time about my feelings
3. Stop forgetting my Algebra notebook
4. Keep my comments to myself
5. Stop writing my Algebra notes in my journal

The 3rd power of x is called cube of x—negative numbers have no sq root

Lilly—I can't stand this. When is she going to go back to the teachers' lounge?

> *Maybe never. I heard they were shampooing the carpet today. God, he is so CUTE.*

Who's cute?

> *BORIS!*

He isn't cute. He's gross. Look what he did to his sweater. Why does he DO that?

> *You're so narrow-minded.*

I am NOT narrow-minded. But someone should tell him that in America we don't tuck in our sweaters.

> *Well, maybe in Russia they do.*

But this isn't Russia. Also, someone should tell him to learn a new song. If I have to hear that requiem for dead King Whoever one more time . . .

> *You're just jealous because Boris is a musical genius and you're flunking Algebra.*

Lilly, just because I am flunking Algebra does NOT mean I'm stupid.

> *OK, OK. What is wrong with you today?*

NOTHING!!!!!

slope: slope of a line denoted m is $m = \dfrac{y2 - y1}{x2 - x1}$

Find equation of line with slope = 2

Find the degree of slope to Mr. G's nostrils

Well.

I guess now I know why my dad is so concerned about not being able to have more kids.

BECAUSE HE'S A PRINCE!!!

Geez! How long did they think they could keep something like *that* from me?

Although, come to think of it, they managed for a pretty long time. I mean, I've BEEN to Genovia. Miragnac, where I go every summer, and also most Christmases, is the name of my grandmother's house in France. It is actually on the border of France, right near Genovia, which is between France and Italy. I've been going to Miragnac ever since I was born. Never with my mother, though. Only with my dad. My mom and dad have never lived together. Unlike a lot of kids I know, who sit around wishing their parents would get back together after they get divorced, I'm perfectly happy with this arrangement. My parents broke up before I was ever born, although they have always been pretty friendly to one another. Except when my dad is being moody, that is, or my mom is being a flake, which she can be sometimes. Things would majorly suck, I think, if they lived together.

Anyway, Genovia is where my grandmother takes me to shop for clothes at the end of every summer, when she's sick of looking at my overalls. But nobody there ever mentioned anything about my dad's being a PRINCE.

Come to think of it, I did that fact sheet on Genovia two years ago, and I copied down the name of the royal family, which is Renaldo. But even then I didn't connect it with my *dad*. I mean, I know his name is Phillipe Renaldo. But the name of the prince of Genovia was listed in the encyclopedia I used as Artur Christoff Phillipe Gerard Grimaldi Renaldo.

And that picture of him must have been totally old. Dad hasn't had any hair since before I was born (so when he had chemo, you couldn't even tell, since he was practically bald anyway). The picture of the prince of Genovia showed someone with A LOT of hair, side-burns, and a mustache, too.

I guess I can see now how Mom might have gone for him, back when she was in college. He was something of a Baldwin.

But a PRINCE? Of a whole COUNTRY? I mean, I knew he was in politics, and of course I knew he had money—how many kids at my school have summer homes in France? Martha's Vineyard, maybe, but not *France*—but a PRINCE?

So what I want to know is, if my dad's a prince, how come I have to learn Algebra?

I mean, seriously.

I don't think it was such a good idea for Dad to tell

me he was a prince in the Palm Court at the Plaza. First of all, we almost had a repeat performance of the shorts incident: The doorman wouldn't even let me in at first. He said, "No minors unaccompanied by an adult," which totally blows that whole *Home Alone II* movie, right?

And I was all, "But I'm supposed to meet my dad—"

"No minors," the doorman said again, "unaccompanied by an adult."

This seemed totally unfair. I wasn't even wearing shorts. I was wearing my uniform from Albert Einstein. I mean, pleated skirt, kneesocks, the whole thing. Okay, maybe I was wearing Doc Martens, but come on! I practically WAS that kid Eloise, and she supposedly ruled the Plaza.

Finally, after standing there for like half an hour, saying, "But my dad . . . but my dad . . . but my dad . . ." the concierge came over and asked, "Just who *is* your father, young lady?"

As soon as I said his name they let me in. I realize now that's because even THEY knew he was a prince. But his own daughter, his own daughter nobody tells!

Dad was waiting at a table. High tea at the Plaza is supposed to be this very big deal. You should *see* all the German tourists snapping pictures of themselves eating chocolate chip scones. Anyway, I used to get a kick out of it when I was a little girl, and since my dad refuses to believe fourteen is not little anymore, we still meet there when he's in town. Oh, we go other places, too. Like we always go to see *Beauty and the Beast*, my all-time favorite Broadway musical, I don't care what Lilly says about Walt Disney and his misogynistic undertones. I've seen it seven times.

So has my dad. His favorite part is when the dancing forks come out.

Anyway, we're sitting there drinking tea and he starts telling me in this very serious voice that he's the prince of Genovia, and then this terrible thing happens:

I get the hiccups.

This only happens when I drink something hot and then eat bread. I don't know why. It had never happened at the Plaza before, but all of a sudden my dad is like, "Mia, I want you to know the truth. I think you're old enough now, and the fact is, now that I can't have any more children, this will have a tremendous impact on your life, and it's only fair I tell you. I am the prince of Genovia."

And I was all, "Really, Dad?" *Hiccup.*

"Your mother has always felt very strongly that there wasn't any reason for you to know, and I agreed with her. I had a very . . . well, *unsatisfactory* childhood—"

He's not kidding. Life with Grandmère couldn't have been any *picque-nicque*. *Hiccup.*

"I agreed with your mother that a palace is no place to raise a child." Then he started muttering to himself, which he always does whenever I tell him I'm a vegetarian, or the subject of Mom comes up. "Of course, at the time I didn't think she intended to raise you in a *bohemian artist's loft* in *Greenwich Village*, but I will admit that it doesn't seem to have done you any harm. In fact, I think growing up in New York City instilled you with a healthy amount of skepticism about the human race at large—"

Hiccup. And he had never even *met* Lana Weinberger.

"—which is something I didn't gain until college, and I believe is partly responsible for the fact that I have such a difficult time establishing close interpersonal relationships with women—"

Hiccup.

"What I'm trying to say is, your mother and I thought by not telling you we were doing you a favor. The fact was, we never envisioned that an occasion might arise in which you might succeed the throne. I was only twenty-five when you were born. I felt certain I would meet another woman, marry her, and have more children. But now, unfortunately, that will never be. So, the fact is, you, Mia, are the heir to the throne of Genovia."

I hiccuped again. This was getting embarrassing. These weren't little ladylike hiccups, either. They were huge, and made my whole body go sproinging up out of my chair like I was some kind of five-foot-nine frog. They were loud, too. I mean *really* loud. The German tourists kept looking over, all giggly and stuff. I knew what my dad was saying was superserious, but I couldn't help it, I just kept hiccuping! I tried holding my breath and counting to thirty—I only got to ten before I hiccuped again. I put a sugar cube on my tongue and let it dissolve. No go. I even tried to scare myself, thinking about my mom and Mr. Gianini French-kissing—even *that* didn't work.

Finally, my dad was like, "Mia? Mia, are you listening? Have you heard a word I said?"

I said, "Dad, can I be excused for a minute?"

He looked sort of pained, like his stomach hurt him, and he slumped back in his chair in this defeated way, but he said, "Go ahead," and gave me five dollars to give to the washroom attendant, which I of course put in my pocket. Five bucks for the washroom attendant! Geez, my whole allowance is ten bucks a week!

I don't know if you've ever been to the ladies' room at the Plaza, but it's like totally the nicest one in Manhattan. It's all pink, and there are mirrors and little couches everywhere, in case you look at yourself and feel the urge to faint from your beauty or something. Anyway, I banged in there, hiccuping like a maniac, and all these women in these fancy hairdos looked up, annoyed at the interruption. I guess I made them mess up their lip liner or something.

I went into one of the stalls, each of which, besides a toilet, has its own private sink with a huge mirror and a dressing table with a little stool with tassels hanging off it. I sat on the stool and concentrated on not hiccuping anymore. Instead, I concentrated on what my dad had said:

He's the prince of Genovia.

A lot of things are beginning to make sense now. Like how when I fly to France I just walk onto the plane from the terminal, but when I get there I'm escorted off the plane before everyone else and get taken away by limo to meet my dad at Miragnac.

I always thought that was because he had frequent flyer privileges.

I guess it's because he's a prince.

And then there's that fact that whenever Grandmère takes me shopping in Genovia she always takes me either before the stores are officially open or after they are officially closed. She calls ahead to ensure we will be let in, and no one has ever said no. In Manhattan, if my mother had tried to do this, the clerks at the Gap would have fallen over from laughing so hard.

And when I'm at Miragnac, I notice that we never go out to eat anywhere. We always have our meals there, or sometimes we go to the neighboring chateau, Mirabeau, which is owned by these nasty British people who have a lot of snotty kids who say things like "That's rot" and "You're a wanker" to one another. One of the younger girls, Nicole, is sort of my friend, but then one night she told me this story about how she was Frenching a boy and I didn't know what Frenching was. I was only eleven at the time, which is no excuse, because so was she. I just thought Frenching was some weird British thing, like toad-in-the-hole, or air raids, or something. So then I mentioned it at the dinner table in front of Nicole's parents, and after that all those kids stopped talking to me.

I wonder if the Brits know that my dad is the prince of Genovia. I bet they do. God, they must have thought I was mentally retarded or something.

Most people have never heard of Genovia. I know when we had to do our fact sheets, none of the other kids ever had. Neither had my mother, she says, before she met my dad. Nobody famous ever came from there. Nobody who was born there ever invented anything, or wrote anything, or became a movie star. A lot of Genovians, like my grandpa, fought against the Nazis in World War II, but other than that, they aren't really known for anything.

Still, people who *have* heard of Genovia like to go there because it's so beautiful. It's very sunny nearly all the time, with the snowcapped Alps in the background and the crystal-blue Mediterranean in front of it. It has a lot of hills, some of which are as steep as the ones in San Francisco, and most of which have olive trees growing on them. The main export of Genovia, I remember from my fact sheet, is olive oil, the really expensive kind my mom says only to use for salad dressing.

There's a palace there, too. It's kind of famous because they filmed a movie there once, a movie about the three Musketeers. I've never been inside, but we've driven by it before, me and Grandmère. It's got all these turrets and flying buttresses and stuff.

Funny how Grandmère never mentioned having *lived* there all those times we drove past it.

My hiccups are gone. I think it's safe to go back to the Palm Court.

I'm going to give the washroom attendant a dollar, even though she didn't attend me.

Hey, I can afford it: My dad's a prince!

I'm so freaked out I can barely write, plus people keep bumping my elbow, and it's dark in here, but whatever. I have to get this down exactly the way it happened. Otherwise, when I wake up tomorrow I might think it was just a nightmare.

But it wasn't a nightmare. It was REAL.

I'm not going to tell anybody, not even Lilly. Lilly would NOT understand. NOBODY would understand. Because nobody I know has ever been in this situation before. Nobody ever went to bed one night as one person and then woke up the next morning to find out that she was somebody completely different.

When I got back to our table after hiccuping in the ladies' room at the Plaza, I saw that the German tourists had been replaced by some Japanese tourists. This was an improvement. They were much quieter. My dad was on his cellular phone when I sat back down. He was talking to my mom, I realized right away. He had on the expression he wears only when he is talking to her. He was saying, "Yes, I told her. No, she doesn't seem upset." He looked at me. "Are you upset?"

I said, "No," because I wasn't upset—not THEN.

He said, into the phone, "She says no." He listened for a minute, then he looked at me again. "Do you want your mother to come up here and help to explain things?"

I shook my head. "No. She has to finish that mixed-media piece for the Kelly Tate Gallery. They want it by next Tuesday."

My dad repeated this to my mom. I heard her grumble back. She is always very grumbly when I remind her that she has paintings due by a certain time. My mom likes to work when the muses move her. Since my dad pays most of our bills, this is not usually a problem, but it is not a very responsible way for an adult to behave, even if she is an artist. I swear, if I ever met my mom's muses, I'd give 'em such swift kicks in the toga they wouldn't know what hit them.

Finally my dad hung up and then he looked at me. "Better?" he asked.

So I guess he had noticed the hiccups after all. "Better," I said.

"Do you really understand what I'm telling you, Mia?"

I nodded. "You are the prince of Genovia."

"Yes . . ." he said, like there was more.

I didn't know what else to say. So I tried, "Grandpère was the prince of Genovia before you?"

He said, "Yes . . ."

"So Grandmère is . . . what?"

"The dowager princess."

I winced. Ew. That explained a whole lot about Grandmère.

Dad could tell he had me stumped. He kept on looking at me all hopeful like. Finally, after I tried just smiling at him innocently for a while, and that didn't work, I slumped over and said, "Okay. What?"

He looked disappointed. "Mia, don't you know?"

I had my head on the table. You aren't supposed to do that at the Plaza, but I hadn't noticed Ivana Trump looking our way. "No . . ." I said. "I guess not. Know what?"

"You're not Mia Thermopolis anymore, honey," he said. Because I was born out of wedlock, and my mom doesn't believe in what she calls the cult of the patriarchy, she gave me her last name instead of my dad's.

I raised my head at that. "I'm not?" I said, blinking a few times. "Then who am I?"

And he went, kind of sadly, "You're Amelia Mignonette Grimaldi Thermopolis Renaldo, Princess of Genovia."

Okay.

WHAT? A PRINCESS?? ME???

Yeah. Right.

This is how NOT a princess I am. I am so NOT a princess that when my dad started telling me that I was one I totally started crying. I could see my reflection in this big gold mirror across the room, and my face had gotten all splotchy, like it does in PE whenever we play dodge ball and I get hit. I looked at my face in that big mirror and I was like, *This* is the face of a princess?

You should see what I look like. You never saw

anyone who looked LESS like a princess than I do. I mean, I have really bad hair that isn't curly or straight; it's sort of triangular, so I have to wear it really short or I look like a Yield sign. And it isn't blond or brunette, it's in the middle, the sort of color they call mouse brown, or dishwater blond. Attractive, huh? And I have a really big mouth and no breasts and feet that look like skis. Lilly says my only attractive feature is my eyes, which are gray, but right then they were all squinty and red-looking since I was trying not to cry.

I mean, princesses don't cry, right?

Then my dad reached out and started patting my hand. Okay, I love my dad, but he just has no clue. He kept saying how sorry he was. I couldn't say anything in reply because I was afraid if I talked I'd cry harder. He kept on saying how it wasn't that bad, that I'd like living at the palace in Genovia with him, and that I could come back to visit my little friends as often as I wanted.

That's when I lost it.

Not only am I a princess, but I have to MOVE???

I stopped crying almost right away. Because then I got mad. Really mad. I don't get mad all that often, because of my fear of confrontation and all, but when I *do* get mad, look out.

"I am NOT moving to Genovia," I said in this really loud voice. I know it was loud because all the Japanese tourists turned around and looked at me, and then started whispering to one another.

My dad looked kind of shocked. The last time I yelled at him had been years ago, when he agreed with Grandmère that I ought to eat some foie gras. I don't care if it *is* a delicacy in France; I'm not eating anything that once walked around and quacked.

"But Mia," my dad said in his Now-let's-be-reasonable voice, "I thought you understood—"

"All I understand," I said, "is that you *lied* to me my whole life. Why should I come live with *you*?"

I realize this was a completely *Party of Five* kind of thing to say, and I'm sorry to say that I followed it up with some pretty *Party of Five* behavior. I stood up real fast, knocking over my big gold chair, and rushed out of there, nearly bowling over the snobby doorman.

I think my dad tried to chase me, but I can run pretty fast when I want to. Mr. Wheeton is always trying to get me to go out for track, but that's like such a joke, because I hate running for no reason. A letter on a stupid jacket is no reason to run, as far as I'm concerned.

Anyway, I ran down the street, past the stupid touristy horses and carriages, past the big fountain with the gold statues in it, past all the traffic outside of F.A.O. Schwarz, right into Central Park, where it was getting kind of dark and cold and spooky and stuff, but I didn't care. Nobody was going to attack me because I was this five-foot-nine girl running in combat boots, with a big backpack with bumper stickers on it that said stuff like SUPPORT GREENPEACE and I BRAKE FOR ANI-MALS. Nobody messes with a girl in combat boots, particularly when she's also a vegetarian.

After a while I got tired of running, and then I tried to figure out where I could go, since I wasn't ready to go home yet. I knew I couldn't go to Lilly's. She is vehemently opposed to any form of government that is not by the people, exercised either directly or through elected representatives. She's always said that when sovereignty is vested in a single person whose right to rule is hereditary, the principles of social equality and respect for the individual within a community are irrevocably lost. This is why, today, real power has passed from reigning monarchs to constitutional assemblies, making royals such as Queen Elizabeth mere symbols of national unity.

At least, that's what she said in her oral report in World Civ the other day.

And I guess I kind of agree with Lilly, especially about Prince Charles—he did treat Diana like dirt—but my dad isn't like that. Yeah, he plays polo and all, but he would never dream of subjecting anyone to taxation without representation.

Still, I was pretty sure the fact that the people of Genovia don't have to pay taxes wasn't going to make any difference to Lilly.

I knew the first thing my dad would do was call Mom, and she'd be all worried. I hate making my mom worry. Even though she can be very irresponsible at times, it's only with things like bills and the groceries. She's never irresponsible about *me*. Like, I have friends whose parents don't even remember sometimes to give them subway fare. I have friends who tell their parents they're going to So-and-So's apartment and then instead they go out drinking, and their parents never find out because they don't even check with the other kid's parents.

My mom's not like that. She ALWAYS checks.

So I knew it wasn't fair to run off like that and make her worry. I didn't care much then about what my dad thought. I was pretty much hating him by then. But I just had to be alone for a little while. I mean, it takes some getting used to, finding out you're a princess. I guess some girls might like it, but not me. I've never been good at girly stuff, you know, like putting on makeup and wearing panty hose and stuff. I mean, I can *do* it, if I have to, but I'd rather not.

Much rather not.

Anyway, I don't know how, but my feet sort of knew where they were going, and before I knew it I was at the zoo.

I love the Central Park Zoo. I always have, since I was a little kid. It's way better than the Bronx Zoo, because it's really small and cozy, and the animals are much friendlier, especially the seals and the polar bears. I love polar bears. At the Central Park Zoo, they have this one polar bear, and all he does all day long is the backstroke. I swear! He was on the news once because this animal psychologist was worried he was under too much stress. It must suck to have people looking at you all day. But then they bought him some toys, and after that he was all right. He just kicks back in his enclosure—they don't have cages at the Central Park Zoo, they have enclosures—and watches you watching him. Sometimes he holds a ball while he does it. I love that bear.

So after I forked over a couple of dollars to get in— that's the other good thing about the zoo: it's cheap—I paid a little call on the polar bear. He appeared to be doing fine. Much better than I was, at the moment. I mean, *his* dad hadn't told him he was the heir to the throne of anywhere. I wondered where that polar bear had come from. I hoped he was from Iceland.

After a while it got too crowded at the polar bear enclosure, so then I went into the penguin house. It smells kind of bad in here, but it's fun. There are these windows that look underwater, so you can see the penguins swimming around, sliding on the rocks and having a good penguin time. Little kids put their hands on the glass, and when a penguin swims toward them, they start screaming. It totally cracks me up. There's a bench you can sit on, too, and that's where I'm sitting now, writing this. You get used to the smell after a while. I guess you can get used to anything.

Oh my God, I can't believe I just wrote that! I will NEVER get used to being Princess Amelia Renaldo! I don't even know who that is! It sounds like the name of some stupid line of makeup, or of somebody from a Disney movie who's been missing and just recovered her memory, or something.

What am I going to do? I CAN'T move to Genovia, I just CAN'T!! Who would look after Fat Louie? My mom can't. She forgets to feed *herself*, let alone a *CAT*.

I'm sure they won't let me have a cat in the palace. At least, not a cat like Louie, who weighs twenty-five pounds and eats socks. He'd scare all the ladies-in-waiting.

Oh, God. *What am I going to do?*

If Lana Weinberger finds out about this, I'm dead.

Of course, I couldn't hide out in the penguin house forever. Eventually, they flicked the lights and said the zoo was closing. I put my journal away and filed out with everybody else. I grabbed a downtown bus and went home, where I was sure I was going to get it BIG TIME from my mom.

What I didn't count on was getting it from BOTH my parents at the same time. This was a first.

"Where have you been, young lady?" my mom wanted to know. She was sitting at the kitchen table with my dad, the telephone between them.

My dad said, at the exact same time, "We were worried sick!"

I thought I was in for the grounding of a lifetime, but all they wanted to know was whether I was all right. I assured them that I was and apologized for going all Jennifer Love Hewitt on them. I just needed to be alone, I said.

I was really worried they'd start in on me, but they totally didn't. My mom did try to make me eat some Ramen, but I wouldn't, because it was beef flavored. And then my dad offered to send his driver to Nobu to pick up some blackened sea bass, but I was like, "Really, Dad, I just want to go to bed." Then my mom started feeling my head and stuff, thinking I was sick. This nearly made me start crying again. I guess my dad recognized my expression from the Plaza, since all of a sudden he was like, "Helen, just leave her alone."

To my surprise, she did. And so I went into my bathroom and closed the door and took a long, hot bath, then got into my favorite pajamas, the cool red flannel ones, found Fat Louie where he was trying to hide under the futon couch (he doesn't like my dad so much), and went to bed.

Before I fell asleep, I could hear my dad talking to my mom in the kitchen for a long, long time. His voice was rumbly, like thunder. It sort of reminded me of Captain Picard's voice on *Star Trek: The Next Generation*.

My dad actually has a lot in common with Captain Picard. You know, he's white and bald and has to rule over a small populace.

Except that Captain Picard always makes everything okay by the end of the episode, and I sincerely doubt everything will be okay for me.

Today when I woke up, the pigeons that live on the fire escape outside my window were cooing away (Fat Louie was on the windowsill—well, as much of him as could fit on the windowsill, anyway—watching them), and the sun was shining, and I actually got up on time and didn't hit the snooze button seven thousand times. I took a shower and didn't cut my legs shaving them, found a fairly unwrinkled blouse at the bottom of my closet, and even got my hair to look sort of halfway passable. I was in a good mood. It was *Friday*. Friday is my favorite day, besides Saturday and Sunday. Fridays always mean two days—two glorious, relaxing days—of NO Algebra are coming my way.

And then I walked out into the kitchen and there was all this pink light coming down through the skylight right on my mom, who was wearing her best kimono and making French toast using Egg Beaters instead of real eggs, even though I'm no longer ovo-lacto since I realized eggs aren't fertilized so they could never have been baby chicks anyway.

And I was all set to thank her for thinking of me, and then I heard this rustle.

And there was my DAD sitting at the dining room table (well, really it's just a table, since we don't have a dining room, but whatever), reading *The New York Times* and wearing a suit.

A *suit*. At seven o'clock in the morning.

And then I remembered. I couldn't believe I'd forgotten it:

I'm a *princess*.

Oh my God. Everything good about my day just went right out the window after that.

As soon as he saw me, my dad was all, "Ah, Mia."

I knew I was in for it. He only says *"Ah, Mia"* when he's about to give me a big lecture.

He folded his paper all carefully and laid it down. My dad always folds papers carefully, making the edges all neat. My mom never does this. She usually crumples the pages up and leaves them, out of order, on the futon couch or next to the toilet. This kind of thing drives my father insane and is probably the real reason why they never got married.

My mom, I saw, had set the table with our best Kmart plates, the ones with the blue stripes on them, and the green plastic cactus-shaped margarita glasses from Ikea. She had even put a bunch of fake sunflowers in the middle of the table in a yellow vase. She had done all that to cheer me up, I know, and she'd probably gotten up really early to do it, too. But instead of cheering me up, it just made me sadder.

Because I bet they don't use green plastic cactus-shaped margarita glasses for breakfast at the palace in Genovia.

"We need to talk, Mia," my dad said. This is how

his worst lectures always start. Except this time he looked at me kind of funny before he started. "What's wrong with your hair?"

I put my hand up to my head. "Why?" I thought my hair looked good, for a change.

"Nothing is wrong with her hair, Phillipe," my mom said. She usually tries to ward off my dad's lectures, if she can. "Come and sit down, Mia, and have some breakfast. I even heated up the syrup for the French toast, the way you like it."

I appreciated this gesture on my mom's part. I really did. But I was not going to sit down and talk about my future in Genovia. I mean, come on. So I was all, "Uh, I'd love to, really, but I gotta go. I have a test in World Civ today, and I promised Lilly I'd meet her to go over our notes together—"

"*Sit down.*"

Boy, my dad can really sound like a starship captain in the Federation when he wants to.

I sat. My mom shoveled some French toast onto my plate. I poured syrup over it and took a bite, just to be polite. It tasted like cardboard.

"Mia," my mom said. She was still trying to ward off my dad's lecture. "I know how upset you must be about all of this. But really, it isn't as bad as you're making it out to be."

Oh, right. All of a sudden you tell me I'm a princess, and I'm supposed to be happy about it?

"I mean," my mom went on, "most girls would probably be delighted to find out their father is a prince!"

No girls I know. Actually, that's not true. Lana Weinberger would probably *love* to be a princess. In fact, she already thinks she is one.

"Just think of all the lovely things you could have if you went to live in Genovia." My mom's face totally lit up as she started listing the lovely things I could have if I went to live in Genovia, but her voice sounded strange, as if she were playing a mom on TV or something. "Like a car! You know how impractical it is to have a car here in the city. But in Genovia, when you turn sixteen, I'm sure Dad will buy you a—"

I pointed out that there are enough problems with pollution in Europe without my contributing to it. Diesel emissions are one of the largest contributors to the destruction of the ozone layer.

"But you've always wanted a horse, haven't you? Well, in Genovia you could have one. A nice gray one with spots on its back—"

That hurt.

"Mom," I said, my eyes all filling up with tears. I completely couldn't help it. Suddenly, I was bawling all over again. "What are you *doing*? Do you *want* me to go live with Dad? Is that it? Are you tired of me or something? Do you want me to go live with Dad so you and Mr. Gianini can . . . can . . ."

I couldn't go on because I started crying so hard. But by then my mom was crying, too. She jumped up out of her chair and came around the end of the table and started hugging me, saying, "Oh, no, honey! How could you think something like that?" She stopped sounding like a TV mom. "I just want what's best for you!"

"As do I," my dad said, looking annoyed. He had folded his arms across his chest and was leaning back in his chair, watching us in an irritated way.

"Well, what's best for me is to stay right here and finish high school," I told him. "And then I'm going to join Greenpeace and help save the whales."

My dad looked even *more* irritated at that. "You are *not* joining Greenpeace," he said.

"I am, too," I said. It was totally hard to talk, because I was crying and all, but I told him, "I'm going to go to Iceland to save the baby seals, too."

"You most certainly are not." My dad didn't just look annoyed. Now he looked mad. "You are going to go to college. Vassar, I think. Maybe Sarah Lawrence."

That made me cry even more.

But before I could say anything, my mom held up a hand and was like, "Phillipe, don't. We aren't accomplishing anything here. Mia has to get to school, anyway. She's already late—"

I started looking around for my backpack and coat real fast. "Yeah," I said. "I gotta renew my MetroCard."

My dad made this weird French noise he makes sometimes. It's halfway between a snort and a sigh. It kind of sounds like *Pfuit!* Then he said, "Lars will drive you."

I told my dad that this was unnecessary since I meet Lilly every day at Astor Place, where we catch the uptown 6 train together.

"Lars can pick up your little friend, too."

I looked at my mom. She was looking at my dad. Lars is my dad's driver. He goes everywhere my dad goes. For as long as I've known my dad—okay, my whole life—he's always had a driver, usually a big beefy guy who used to work for the president of Israel or somebody like that.

Now that I think about it, of course I realize these guys aren't really drivers at all but bodyguards.

Duh.

Okay, so the last thing I wanted was for my dad's bodyguard to drive me to school. How would I ever explain it to Lilly? *Oh, don't mind him, Lilly. He's just my dad's chauffeur.* Yeah, right. The only person at Albert Einstein High School who gets dropped off by a chauffeur is this totally rich Saudi Arabian girl named Tina Hakim Baba, whose dad owns some big oil company, and everybody makes fun of her because her parents are all worried she'll get kidnapped between Seventy-fifth and Madison, where our school is, and Seventy-fifth and Fifth, where she lives. She even has a bodyguard who follows her around from class to class and talks on a walkie-talkie to the chauffeur. This seems a little extreme, if you ask me.

But Dad was totally rigid on the driver thing. It's like now that I'm an official princess there's all this concern for my welfare. Yesterday, when I was Mia Thermopolis, it was perfectly okay for me to ride the subway. Today, now that I'm Princess Amelia, forget it.

Well, whatever. It didn't seem worth arguing over. I mean, there are way worse things I have to worry about.

Like which country am I going to be living in in the near future.

As I was leaving—my dad made Lars come up to the loft to walk me down to the car; it was totally embarrassing—I overheard my dad say to my mom, "All right, Helen. Who's this Gianini fellow Mia was talking about?"

Oops.

$ab = a + b$
solve for b
$ab - b = a$
$b(a - 1) = a$
$b = \dfrac{a}{a - 1}$

Lilly could tell right away something was up.

Oh, she swallowed the whole story I fed her about Lars: "Oh, my dad's in town, and he's got this driver, and you know . . ."

But I couldn't tell her about the princess thing. I mean, all I kept thinking about was how disgusted Lilly sounded during that part in her oral report when she mentioned how Christian monarchs used to consider themselves appointed agents of divine will and thus were responsible not to the people they governed but to God alone, even though my dad hardly ever even goes to church, except when Grandmère makes him.

Lilly believed me about Lars, but she was still all over me with the crying thing. She was like, "Why are your eyes so red and squinty? You've been crying. Why were you crying? Did something happen? What happened? Did you get another F in something?"

I just shrugged and tried to look out the passenger window at the uninspiring view of the East Village crackhouses, which we had to drive by to get to the FDR. "It's nothing," I said. "PMS."

"It is not PMS. You had your period last week. I remember because you borrowed a pad from me after PE, and then you ate two whole packs of Yodels at lunch." Sometimes I wish Lilly's memory weren't so good. "So spill. Did Louie eat another sock?"

First of all, it was like totally embarrassing to discuss my menstrual cycle in front of my dad's bodyguard. I mean, Lars is kind of a Baldwin. He was concentrating really hard on driving, though, and I don't know if he could hear us from the front seat, but it was embarrassing, just the same.

"It's nothing," I whispered. "Just my dad. *You know.*"

"Oh," Lilly said in her normal voice. Have I mentioned that Lilly's normal voice is really loud? "You mean the infertility thing? Is he still bummed out about that? Gawd, does *he* ever need to self-actualize."

Lilly then went on to describe something she called the Jungian tree of self-actualization. She says my dad is way on the bottom branches, and he won't be able to reach the top of the thing until he accepts himself as he is and stops obsessing over his inability to sire more offspring.

I guess that's part of my problem. I'm way at the bottom of the self-actualization tree. Like, underneath the roots of it, practically.

But now that I'm sitting here in Algebra, things don't seem so bad, really. I mean, I thought about it all through Homeroom, and I finally realized something:

They can't *make* me be princess.

They really can't. I mean, this is America, for crying out loud. Here, you can be anything you want to be. At least that's what Mrs. Holland was always telling us last year, when we studied U.S. History. So, if I can be whatever I want to be, I can *not* be a princess.

Nobody can *make* me be a princess, not even my dad, if I don't want to be one.

Right?

So when I get home tonight, I'll just tell my dad thanks, but no thanks. I'll just be plain old Mia for now.

Geez. Mr. Gianini just called on me, and I totally had no idea what he was talking about, because of course I was writing in this book instead of paying attention. My face feels like it's on fire. Lana is laughing her head off, of course. She is such a wanker.

What does he keep picking on *me* for, anyway? He should know by now that I don't know the quadratic formula from a hole in the ground. He's only picking on me because of my mom. He wants to make it look as if he's treating me the same as everybody else in the class.

Well, I'm *not* the same as everybody else in the class.

What do I need to know Algebra for, anyway? They don't use Algebra in Greenpeace.

And you can bet you don't need it if you're a princess. So however things turn out, I'm covered.

Cool.

solve $x = a + aby$ for y

$x - a = aby$

$\dfrac{x - a}{ab} = \dfrac{aby}{ab}$

$\dfrac{x - a}{ab} = y$

Really Late on Friday, Lilly Moscovitz's Bedroom

Okay, so I blew off Mr. Gianini's help session after school. I *know* I shouldn't have. Believe me, Lilly let me know I shouldn't have. I know he has these help sessions just for people like me, who are flunking. I know he does it in his own spare time and doesn't even get paid overtime for it or anything. But if I won't ever need Algebra in any foreseeable future career, why do I need to go?

I asked Lilly if it would be okay if I spent the night at her house tonight and she said only if I promised to stop acting like such a head case.

I promised, even though I don't think I'm acting like a head case.

But when I called my mom from the pay phone in the lobby after school to ask her if it was okay if I stayed overnight at the Moscovitzes, she was all, "Um, actually, Mia, your father was really hoping that when you got home tonight we could have another talk."

Oh, great.

I told my mom that although there was nothing I wanted to do more than have another talk, I was very concerned about Lilly, whose stalker was recently released from Bellevue again. Ever since Lilly started her cable access TV show, this guy named Norman has been calling in, asking her to take off her shoes.

According to the Drs. Moscovitz, Norman is a fetishist. His fixation is feet—in particular, Lilly's feet. He sends stuff to her care of the show, CDs and stuffed animals and things like that, and writes that there'll be more where that came from if Lilly would just take off her shoes on air. So what Lilly does is, she takes off her shoes, all right, but then she throws a blanket over her legs and kicks her feet around under it and goes, "Look, Norman, you freak! I took my shoes off! Thanks for the CDs, sucker!"

This angered Norman so much that he started wandering around the Village looking for Lilly. Everyone knows Lilly lives in the Village, since we filmed a very popular episode where Lilly borrowed the pricing gun from Grand Union and stood on the corner of Bleecker and La Guardia and told all the European tourists wandering around NoHo that if they wore a Grand Union price sticker on their foreheads they could get a free latte from Dean & DeLuca (a surprising amount of them believed her).

Anyway, one day a few weeks ago Norman the foot fetishist found us in the park and started chasing us around, waving twenty dollar bills and trying to get us to take off our shoes. This was very entertaining, and hardly scary at all, especially because we just ran right up to the command post on Washington Square South and Thompson Street, where the Sixth Precinct has been parking this enormous trailer so they can secretly spy on the drug dealers. We told the police that this weird guy was trying to assault us, and you should have seen it: About twenty undercover guys (even a guy I thought was an old homeless man asleep on a bench) jumped on Norman and dragged him, screaming, off to the mental ward!

I always have such a good time with Lilly.

Anyway, Lilly's parents told her Norman just got out of Bellevue and that if she sees him she's not to torment him anymore, because he's just a poor obsessive-compulsive with possible schizophrenic tendencies.

Lilly's devoting tomorrow's show to her feet. She's going to model every single pair of shoes she owns, but not once show her bare feet. She hopes that this will drive Norman over the edge and he'll do something weirder than ever, like get a gun and shoot at us.

I'm not scared, though. Norman has kind of thick glasses, and I bet he couldn't actually hit anything, even with a machine gun, which even a lunatic like Norman is allowed to buy in this country thanks to our totally unrestrictive gun laws, which Michael Moscovitz says in his webzine will ultimately result in the demise of democracy as we know it.

My mom was totally not buying this, though. She was all, "Mia, I appreciate the fact that you want to help your friend through this difficult period with her stalker, but I really think you have more pressing responsibilities here at home."

And I was all, "What responsibilities?" thinking she was talking about the litter box, which I had totally cleaned two days ago.

And she was like, "Responsibility toward your father and me."

I just about lost it right there. Responsibilities? *Responsibilities? She's* telling *me* about responsibilities? When is the last time it ever occurred to *her* to drop off the laundry, let alone pick it up again? When is the last time *she* remembered to buy Q-Tips or toilet paper or milk?

And did she ever happen to think to mention, in all of my fourteen years, that I might possibly end up being the princess of Genovia someday???

She thinks she needs to tell *me* about my responsibilities?

HA!!!!!!

I nearly hung up on her. But Lilly was sort of standing nearby, practicing her house manager duties by switching on and off the lights in the school lobby. Since I had promised not to act like a head case, and hanging up on my mother would definitely fall into the head case category, I said in this really patient voice, "Don't worry, Mom, I won't forget to stop at Genovese on my way home tomorrow and pick up new vacuum cleaner bags."

And *then* I hung up.

HOMEWORK

Algebra: problems 1–12, pg. 119
English: proposal
World Civ: questions at end of Chapter 4
G&T: none
French: use *avoir* in neg. sentence, rd. lessons one to three, pas de plus
Biology: none

Why do I always have such a good time when I spend the night at Lilly's? I mean, it's not like they've got stuff that I don't have. In fact, my mom and I have better stuff. The Moscovitzes only get a couple of movie channels, and because I took advantage of the last Time Warner Cable bonus offer, we have all of them, Cinemax *and* HBO *and* Showtime, for the low, low rate of $19.99 per month.

Plus we have way better people to spy on through our windows, like Ronnie, who used to be a Ronald but is now called Ronette, and who has a lot of big fancy parties; and that skinny German couple who wear black all the time, even in summer, and never pull down their blinds. On Fifth Avenue, where the Moscovitzes live, there's *nobody* good to look at: Just other rich psychoanalysts and their children. Let me tell you, you don't see anything good through *their* windows.

But it's like every time I spend the night here, even if all Lilly and I do is hang out in the kitchen eating macaroons left over from Rosh Hashanah, I have such a great time. Maybe that's because Maya, the Moscovitzes' Dominican maid, never forgets to buy orange juice, and she always remembers that I don't like the pulpy kind, and sometimes, if she knows I'm staying over, she'll pick up a vegetable lasagna from Balducci's, instead of a meat one, especially for me, like she did last night.

Or maybe it's because I never find moldy old containers of anything in the Moscovitzes' refrigerator. Maya throws away anything that's even one day past its expiration date. Even sour cream that still has the protective plastic around the lid. Even cans of Tab.

And the Drs. Moscovitz never forget to pay the electricity bill. Con Ed has never once shut down *their* power in the middle of a *Star Trek* movie marathon. And Lilly's mom, she always talks about normal stuff, like what a great deal she got on Calvin Klein panty hose at Bergdorf's.

Not that I don't love my mom or anything. I totally do. I just wish she could be more of a mom and less of an artist.

And I wish my dad could be more like Lilly's dad, who always wants to make me an omelet because he thinks I'm too skinny, and who walks around in his old college sweatpants when he doesn't have to go to his office to analyze anybody.

Dr. Moscovitz would *never* wear a suit at seven in the morning.

Not that I don't love my dad. I do, I guess. I just don't understand how he could let something like this happen. He's usually so organized. *How could he have let himself become a prince?*

I just don't understand it.

The best thing, I guess, about going to Lilly's is that while I'm there I don't even have to think about things like how I'm flunking Algebra or how I'm the heir to the throne of a small European principality. I can just relax and enjoy some real homemade Poppin Fresh Cinnamon Buns and watch Pavlov, Michael's sheltie, try to herd Maya back into the kitchen every time she tries to come out.

Last night was *totally* fun. The Drs. Moscovitz were out—they had to go to a benefit at the Puck Building for the homosexual children of survivors of the Holocaust—so Lilly and I made this huge vat of popcorn smothered in butter and climbed into her parents' giant canopy bed and watched all the James Bond movies in a row. We were able to definitively determine that Pierce Brosnan was the skinniest James Bond, Sean Connery the hairiest, and Roger Moore the most tan. None of the James Bonds took off their shirts enough for us to decide who had the best chest, but I think probably Timothy Dalton.

I like chest hair. I think.

It was sort of ironic that while I was trying to decide this Lilly's brother came into the room. He had on a shirt, though. He looked kind of annoyed. He said my dad was on the phone. My dad was all mad because he'd been trying to get through for hours, only Michael was on the Internet answering fan mail for his webzine, *Crackhead*, so my dad kept getting a busy signal.

I must have looked like I was going to throw up or something, because after a minute Michael said, "Okay, don't worry about it, Thermopolis. I'll tell him you and Lilly already went to bed," which is a lie my mother would never believe, but it must have gone over pretty well with my dad, since Michael came back and reported that my dad had apologized for calling so late (it was only eleven) and that he'd speak to me in the morning.

Great. I can't wait.

I guess I must have still looked like I was going to throw up, because Michael called his dog and made him get into bed with us, even though pets aren't allowed in the Drs. Moscovitzes' room. Pavlov crawled into my lap and started licking my face, which he'll only do to people he really trusts. Then Michael sat down to watch the movies with us, and in the interest of science, Lilly asked him which Bond girls were most attractive to him, the blonds who always needed James Bond to rescue them or the brunettes who were always pulling guns on him, and Michael said he couldn't resist a girl with a weapon, which got us started on his two favorite TV shows of all time, *Xena: Warrior Princess* and *Buffy the Vampire Slayer*.

So then, not really in the interest of science but more out of plain curiosity, I asked Michael if it was the end of the world and he had to repopulate the planet but he could only choose one life mate, who would it be, Xena or Buffy?

After telling me how weird I was for thinking of something like that, Michael chose Buffy, and then Lilly asked me if I had to choose between Harrison Ford or George Clooney who would it be, and I said Harrison Ford even though he's so old, but the Harrison Ford from *Indiana Jones*, not *Star Wars*, and then Lilly said she'd choose Harrison Ford as Jack Ryan in those Tom Clancy movies, and then Michael goes, "Who would you choose, Harrison Ford or Leonardo DiCaprio?" and we both chose Harrison Ford because Leonardo is so passé, and then he went, "Who would you choose, Harrison Ford or Josh Richter?" and Lilly said Harrison Ford, because he used to be a carpenter, and if it was the end of the world he could build her a house, but I said Josh Richter, because he'd live longer—Harrison is like SIXTY—and be able to give me a hand with the kids.

Then Michael started saying all this totally unfair stuff about Josh Richter, like how in the face of nuclear Armageddon he'd probably show cowardice, but Lilly said fear of new things is not an accurate measure of one's potential for growth, with which I agreed. Then Michael said we were both idiots if we thought Josh Richter would ever give us so much as the time of day, that he only liked girls like Lana Weinberger, who put out, to which Lilly responded that she would put out for Josh Richter if he was able to meet certain conditions, like bathing beforehand in an antibacterial solution and wearing three condoms coated in spermicidal fluid during the act, in case one broke and one slipped off.

Then Michael asked me if I would put out for Josh Richter, and I had to think about it for a minute. Losing your virginity is a really big step, and you have to do it with the right person or else you could be screwed up for the rest of your life, like the women in Dr. Moscovitz's Over Forty and Still Single group, which meets every other Tuesday. So after I'd thought about it, I said I would put out for Josh Richter, but only if:

1. We'd been dating for at least a year.
2. He pledged his undying love to me.
3. He took me to see *Beauty and the Beast* on Broadway and didn't make fun of it.

Michael said the first two sounded all right, but if the third one was an example of the kind of boyfriend I expected to get, I'd be a virgin for a long, long time. He said he didn't know anyone with an ounce of testosterone who could watch *Beauty and the Beast* on Broadway without projectile vomiting. But he's wrong, because my dad definitely has testosterone—at least one testicle full—and he's never projectile vomited at the show.

Then Lilly asked Michael who he would choose if he had to, me or Lana Weinberger, and he said, "Mia, of course," but I'm sure he was just saying that because I was right there in the room and he didn't want to dis me to my face.

I wish Lilly wouldn't do things like that.

But she kept on doing it, wanting to know who Michael would choose, me or Madonna, and me or Buffy the Vampire Slayer (he chose me over Madonna, but Buffy won, hands down, over me).

And then Lilly wanted to know who I would choose, Michael or Josh Richter. I pretended to be seriously thinking about it, when to my total relief the Drs. Moscovitz came home and started yelling at us for letting Pavlov in their room and eating popcorn in their bed.

So then later after Lilly and I had cleaned up all the popcorn and gone back to her room, she asked me again who I would choose, Josh Richter or her brother, and I had to say Josh Richter, because Josh Richter is the hottest boy in our whole school, maybe the whole world, and I am completely and totally in love with him, and not just because of the way his blond hair sometimes falls into his eyes when he's bent over, looking for stuff in his locker, but because I know that behind that jock facade he maintains he is a deeply sensitive and caring person. I could tell by the way he said hey to me that day in Bigelows.

But I couldn't help thinking if it *really* were the end of the world, it might be better to be with Michael, even if he isn't so hot, because at least he makes me laugh. I think at the end of the world a sense of humor would be important.

Plus, of course, Michael looks really good without a shirt.

And if it really was the end of the world, Lilly would be dead, so she'd never know her brother and I were procreating!

I'd *never* want Lilly to know that I feel that way about her brother. She'd think it was weird.

Weirder even than me turning out to be the princess of Genovia.

Later on Saturday

The whole way home from Lilly's I worried about what my mom and dad were going to say when I got home. I had never disobeyed them before. I mean, really never.

Well, okay, there was that one time Lilly and Shameeka and Ling Su and I went to see that Christian Slater movie, but we ended up going to *The Rocky Horror Picture Show* instead, and I forgot to call until after the movie, which ended at like 2:30 in the morning and we were in Times Square and didn't have enough money left among us for a cab.

But that was just that one time! And I totally learned a lesson from it, without my mom having to ground me or anything. Not that she would ever do something like that—ground me, I mean. Who would go to the cash machine to get money for takeout if I were grounded?

But my dad's another story. He is totally rigid in the discipline department. My mom says that's because Grandmère used to punish him when he was a little boy by locking him into this one really scary room in their house.

Now that I think about it, the house my dad grew up in was probably the castle, and that scary room was probably the dungeon.

Geez, no wonder my dad does every single thing Grandmère says.

Anyway, when my dad gets mad at me he *really* gets mad. Like the time I wouldn't go to church with Grandmère because I refused to pray to a god who would allow rain forests to be destroyed in order to make grazing room for cows who would later become Quarter Pounders for the ignorant masses who worship that symbol of all that is evil, Ronald McDonald. Not only did my dad tell me that if I didn't go to church he'd wear out my behind, he said he wouldn't let me read Michael's webzine, *Crackhead*, again! He refused to let me go online again for the rest of the summer. He crushed my modem with a magnum of Chateauneuf du Pape.

Talk about reactionary!

So I was totally worried about what he was going to do when I got home from Lilly's.

I tried to hang out at the Moscovitzes' as long as possible: I loaded the breakfast dishes in the dishwasher for Maya, since she was busy writing a letter to her congressman asking him to please do something about her son, Manuel, who was wrongfully imprisoned ten years ago for supporting a revolution in their country. I walked Pavlov, since Michael had to go to an astrophysics lecture at Columbia. I even unclogged the jets in the Drs. Moscovitzes' Jacuzzi—boy, does Lilly's dad shed a lot.

Then Lilly had to go and announce that it was time to shoot the one-hour special episode of her show, the one dedicated to her feet. Only it turned out the Drs.

Moscovitz had not left, like we thought they had, for their rolfing sessions. They totally overheard and told me that I had to go home while they analyzed Lilly about her need to taunt her sex-crazed stalker.

Here's the thing:

I am generally a very good daughter. I mean it. I don't smoke. I don't do drugs. I haven't given birth at any proms. I am completely trustworthy, and I do my homework most of the time. Except for one lousy F in a class that will be of no use to me whatsoever in my future life, I'm doing pretty well.

And then they had to spring the princess thing on me.

I decided on my way home that if my dad tried to punish me I was going to call Judge Judy. He'd really be sorry if he landed in front of Judge Judy because of this. She'd let him have it, boy, let me tell you. People trying to make other people be princesses when they don't want to be? Judge Judy wouldn't stand for any of it.

Of course, when I got home, it turned out I didn't have to call Judge Judy at all.

My mom hadn't gone to her studio, which she does every Saturday without fail. She was sitting there waiting for me to come home, reading old copies of the subscription she got me to *Seventeen* magazine before she realized I was too flat-chested to ever be asked out on a date, so all the information provided in that particular periodical was worthless to me.

Then there was my dad, who was sitting in the exact

same spot as he'd been when I'd left the day before, only this time he was reading the *Sunday Times*, even though it was Saturday, and Mom and I have this rule that you can't start reading the Sunday sections until Sunday. To my surprise, he wasn't wearing a suit. Today he had on a sweater—cashmere, no doubt given to him by one of his many girlfriends—and corduroy pants.

When I walked in, he folded the paper all carefully, put it down, and gave me this long, intent look, like Captain Picard right before he starts going on to Riker about the Prime Directive. Then he goes, "We need to talk."

I immediately started in about how it wasn't like I hadn't told them where I was, and how I just needed a little time away to think about things, and how I'd been really careful and hadn't taken the subway or anything, and my dad just went, "I know."

Just like that. "*I know.*" He completely gave in without a fight.

My dad.

I looked at my mom to see if she'd noticed that he'd lost his mind. And then she did the craziest thing. She put the magazine down and came over and hugged me and said, "We're so sorry, baby."

Hello? These are my *parents?* Did the body snatchers come while I was gone and replace my parents with pod people? Because that was the only way I could think of that my parents would be so reasonable.

Then my dad goes, "We understand the stress that this has brought you, Mia, and we want you to know that we'll do everything in our power to try to make this transition as smooth for you as possible."

Then my dad asked me if I knew what a compromise was, and I said yes, of course, I'm not in like the third grade anymore, so he pulled out this piece of paper, and on it we all drafted what my mom calls the Thermopolis-Renaldo Compromise. It goes like this:

> *I, the undersigned, Artur Christoff Phillipe Gerard Grimaldi Renaldo, agree that my sole offspring and heir, Amelia Mignonette Grimaldi Thermopolis Renaldo, may finish out her high school tenure at Albert Einstein School for Boys (made coeducational circa 1975) without interruption, save for Christmas and summer breaks, which she will spend without complaint in the country of Genovia.*

I asked if that meant no more summers at Miragnac, and he said yes. I couldn't believe it. Christmas and summer, free of Grandmère? That would be like going to the dentist, only instead of having cavities filled I'd just get to read *Teen People* and suck up a lot of laughing gas! I was so happy, I hugged him right there. But unfortunately, it turned out there was more to the agreement:

*I, the undersigned, Amelia Mignonette
Grimaldi Thermopolis Renaldo, agree to
fulfill the duties of heir to Artur Christoff
Phillipe Gerard Grimaldi Renaldo, prince
of Genovia, and all that such a role entails,
including but not exclusive to, assuming the
throne upon the latter's demise and attending
functions of state at which the presence of said
heir is deemed essential.*

All of that sounded pretty good to me, except the
last part. Functions of state? What were they?

My dad got all vague: "Oh, you know. Attending
the funerals of world leaders, opening balls, that sort of
thing."

Hello? Funerals? Balls? Whatever happened to
smashing bottles of champagne against ocean liners, and
going to Hollywood premieres, and that kind of thing?

"Well," my dad said, "Hollywood premieres aren't
really all they're pegged up to be. Flashbulbs going off
in your face, that kind of thing. Terribly unpleasant."

Yeah, but *funerals? Balls?* I don't even know how to
put on lip liner, let alone curtsy. . . .

"Oh, that's all right," my dad said, putting the cap
back on his pen. "Grandmère will take care of that."

Yeah, right. What can *she* do? She's in France!

Ha! Ha! Ha!

Saturday Night

I can't even believe what a loser I am. I mean, Saturday night, alone with my DAD!

He actually tried to talk me into going to see *Beauty and the Beast*, like he felt sorry for me because I didn't have a date!

I finally had to say, "Look, Dad, I am not a child anymore. Even the prince of Genovia can't get tickets to a Broadway show at a minute's notice on a Saturday night."

He was just feeling left out because Mom had taken off on another date with Mr. Gianini. She wanted to cancel on him, given all the upheaval that has occurred in my life over the past twenty-four hours, but I totally made her go because I could see her lips getting smaller and smaller the more time she spent with Dad. Mom's lips only get small when she's trying to keep herself from saying something, and I think what she wanted to say to my dad was *"Get out! Go back to your hotel! You're paying six hundred dollars a night for that suite! Can't you go stay in it?"*

My dad drives my mom completely insane because he's always going around, digging her bank statements out from the big salad bowl where she throws all our mail, and trying to tell her how much she would save in interest if she would just transfer funds out of her checking account and into a Roth IRA.

So even though she felt like she should stay home, I knew if she did she'd explode, so I said go, please go, and that Dad and I would discuss what it's like to govern a small principality in today's economic market. Only when Mom came out in her datewear, which included this totally hot black minidress from Victoria's Secret (my mom hates shopping, so she buys all her clothes from catalogs while she's soaking in the tub after a long day of painting), my dad started to choke on this ice cube. I guess he had never seen my mom in a minidress before—back in college, when they were going out, all she ever wore were overalls, like me—because he drank down his scotch and soda really fast and then said, "*That's* what you're wearing?" which made my mom go, "What's wrong with it?" and look at herself all worriedly in the mirror.

She looked totally fine; in fact, she looked much better than she usually did, which I guess was the problem. I mean, it sounds weird to admit, but my mom can be a total Betty when she puts her mind to it. I can only *wish* that someday I'll be as pretty as my mom. I mean, *she* doesn't have Yield sign hair or a flat chest or size-ten shoes. She is way hot, as far as moms go.

Then the buzzer rang and Mom ran out because she didn't want Mr. Gianini to come up and meet her ex, the prince of Genovia. Which was understandable, since he was still choking and looked sort of funny. I mean, he looked like a red-faced bald man in a cashmere sweater coughing up a lung. I mean, *I* would have been embarrassed to admit I had ever had sex with him, if I were her.

Anyway, it was good for me that she didn't buzz Mr. Gianini up, because I didn't want him asking me in front of my parents why I hadn't gone to his review session on Friday.

So then, after they were gone, I tried to show my dad how much better suited I am for life in Manhattan than in Genovia by ordering some really excellent food. I got us an insalata caprese, ravioli al funghetto, and a pizza margherita, all for under twenty bucks, but I swear, my dad wasn't a bit impressed! He just poured himself another scotch and soda and turned on the TV. He didn't even notice when Fat Louie sat down next to him. He started petting him like it was nothing. And my dad claims to be *allergic* to cats.

And then, to top it all off, he didn't even want to talk about Genovia. All he wanted to do was watch sports. I'm not kidding. Sports. We have seventy-seven channels, and all he would watch were the ones showing men in uniforms chasing after a little ball. Forget the Dirty Harry movie marathon. Forget Pop-Up Videos. He just turned on the sports channel and stared at it, and when I happened to mention that Mom and I usually watch whatever is on HBO on Saturday nights, he just turned up the volume!!!

What a baby.

And you think that's bad? You should have seen him when the food got here. He made Lars frisk the deliveryman before he would let me buzz him up! Can you believe it? I had to give Antonio a whole extra dollar to make up for the indignity of it all. And then my dad sat down and ate, without saying a word, until, after another scotch and soda, he fell asleep, right on the futon, with Fat Louie on his lap!

I guess being a prince and having had testicular cancer can really make a person think he's something special. I mean, God forbid he should share some quality time with his only daughter, the heir to his throne.

So here I am again, home on a Saturday night. Not that I'm ever NOT home on a Saturday night, except when I'm with Lilly. Why am I so unpopular? I mean, I know I look weird and stuff, but I really try to be nice to people, you know? You'd think people would value me as a human being and invite me to their parties just because they like my company. It's not MY fault my hair sticks out the way it does, any more than it's Lilly's fault her face looks sort of squished.

I tried to call Lilly a zillion times, but her phone was busy, which meant Michael was probably home working on his 'zine. The Moscovitzes are trying to have a second line installed so that people who call them can actually get through once in a while, but the phone company says it doesn't have any more 212 numbers to give out. Lilly's mom says she refuses to have two separate area codes in the same apartment and that if she can't have 212 she'll just buy a beeper. Besides, Michael will be leaving for college next fall, and then their phone problems will be solved.

I really wanted to talk to Lilly. I mean, I haven't told her anything about the princess thing, and I'm not going to, *ever*, but sometimes, even without telling her what's bothering me, talking to Lilly makes me feel better. Maybe it's just knowing that somebody else my age is also stuck at home on a Saturday night. I mean, most of the other girls in our class date. Even Shameeka has started dating. She's been quite popular since she developed breasts over the summer. True, her curfew is ten o'clock, even on weekends, and she has to introduce her date to her mom and dad, and her date has to provide a detailed itinerary of exactly where they're going and what they'll be doing, besides showing two pieces of photo ID for Mr. Taylor to photocopy before he'll let Shameeka go out of the house with him.

But still, she's *dating*. Somebody *asked her out*.

Nobody has ever asked me out.

It was pretty boring, watching my dad snore, even though it was fairly comical the way Fat Louie kept glancing at him, all annoyed, every time he inhaled. I had already seen all the Dirty Harry movies, and there was nothing else on. I decided to try instant messaging Michael, telling him I really needed to talk to Lilly and would he please go off-line so I could call her.

CRACKING: What do you want, Thermopolis?

FTLOUIE: I want to talk to Lilly. Please go off-line so I can call her.

CRACKING: What do you want to talk to her about?

FTLOUIE: None of your business. Just go off-line, please. You can't hog all the lines of communication to yourself. It isn't fair.

CRACKING: No one ever said life was fair, Thermopolis. What are you doing home, anyway? What's the matter? Dreamboy didn't call?

FTLOUIE: Who's Dreamboy?

CRACKING: You know, your postnuclear Armageddon life-mate of choice, Josh Richter.

Lilly told him! I can't believe she told him! I'm going to kill her.

FTLOUIE: Would you please go off-line so I can call Lilly????

CRACKING: What's the matter, Thermopolis? Did I strike a nerve?

I logged off. He can be such a jerk sometimes.

But then about five minutes later the phone rang, and it was Lilly. So I guess even though Michael's a jerk, he can be a nice jerk when he wants to be.

Lilly's very upset about how her parents are violating her First Amendment right to free speech by not letting her make the episode of her show dedicated to her feet. She is going to call the ACLU as soon as it opens on Monday morning. Without her parents' financial support, which they have currently revoked, *Lilly Tells It Like It Is* cannot go on. It costs about $200 per episode, if you include the cost of tape and all. Public access is only accessible to people with cash.

Lilly was so upset that I didn't feel like yelling at her about telling Michael that I chose Josh. Now that I think about it, it's probably just better that way.

My life is a convoluted web of lies.

I can't believe Mr. Gianini told her. I can't believe he told my mother I skipped his stupid review session on Friday!!!!

Hello? Do I have no rights here? Can't I skip a review session and not get finked on by my mother's boyfriend?

I mean, it's not like my life isn't bad enough: I'm already deformed, *and* I have to be a princess. Do I have to have my every activity reported upon by my Algebra teacher????

Thanks a lot, Mr. Gianini. Thanks to you, I got to spend my entire Sunday having the quadratic formula drilled into me by my demented father, who kept rubbing his bald head and screaming in frustration when he found out I don't know how to multiply fractions.

Hello? May I remind everyone that I'm supposed to have Saturday and Sunday OFF from school?

AND Mr. Gianini had to go and tell my mother there's going to be a pop quiz tomorrow. I mean, I guess that was kind of nice of him and all, to give me a heads-up, but you're not supposed to study for a pop quiz. The whole point is to test what you've retained.

Then again, since I've apparently retained nothing mathematical since about the second grade, I guess I can't really blame my dad for being so mad. He said if I don't pass Algebra he's going to make me go to summer school. So then I pointed out that summer school was fine by me, since I'd already agreed to spend summers in Genovia. So then he said I'd have to go to summer school in GENOVIA!

I am so sure. I met some kids who went to school in Genovia and they didn't even know what a number line was. And they measure everything by kilos and centimeters. As if metric wasn't so totally over!

But just in case, I'm not taking any chances. I wrote out the quadratic formula on the white rubber sole of my Converse high-top, right where it curves in between my heel and my toes. I'll wear them tomorrow and cross my legs and take a peek if I get stuck.

Monday, October 6, 3 a.m.

I've been up all night, worrying about getting caught cheating. What will happen if someone sees I have the quadratic formula written on my shoe? Will I be expelled? I don't want to be expelled! I mean, even though everybody at Albert Einstein High School thinks I'm a freak, I'm sort of getting used to it. I don't want to have to start over at a whole new school. I'll have to wear the scarlet mark of being a cheater for the rest of my high school career!

And what about college? I might not get into college if it goes down on my permanent record that I'm a cheater.

Not that I want to go to college. But what about Greenpeace? I'm sure Greenpeace doesn't want cheaters. Oh my God, what am I going to do???

Monday, October 6, 4 a.m.

I tried washing the quadratic formula off my shoe, but it won't come off! I must have used indelible ink or something! What if my dad finds out? Do they still behead people in Genovia?

Monday, October 6, 7 a.m.

Decided to wear my Docs and throw my high-tops away on the way to school—but then I broke one of the bootlaces! I can't wear any of my other shoes because they're all size nine and a half, and my foot grew a whole half inch last month! I can barely walk in my loafers, and my heels hang out over the backs of my clogs. I have no choice but to wear my high-tops!

I'm going to get caught for sure, I just know it.

Monday, October 6, 9 a.m.

Realized in the car on the way to school that I could have taken the laces out of my high-tops and strung them through my Doc Martens. I am so stupid.

Lilly wants to know how much longer my dad is going to be in town. She doesn't like being driven to school. She likes to ride the subway, because then she can brush up on her Spanish, by reading all the health awareness posters. I told her I didn't know how long my dad was going to be in town, but that I had a feeling I wasn't going to be allowed to ride the subway anymore, anywhere.

Lilly observed that my father was taking this infertility thing too far, that just because he can no longer render anyone *embarrazada* is no reason to get all overprotective of me. I noticed that, in the driver's seat, Lars was sort of laughing to himself. I hope he doesn't speak Spanish. How embarrassing.

Anyway, Lilly went on to say I should take a stand right away, now, before things get worse, and that she could tell it was already starting to take a toll on me, since I seemed listless and there were circles under my eyes.

Of course I'm listless! I've been up since 3 A.M., trying to wash my shoes!

Went into the girls' room to try to wash them again. Lana Weinberger came in while I was there. She saw me washing my shoes, and she just rolled her eyes and started brushing her long, Marcia Brady hair and staring at herself in the mirror. I half expected her to walk right up to her reflection and kiss it, she is so obviously in love with herself.

The quadratic formula is smeared, but still legible, on my sneaker. But I won't look at it during the test, I swear.

Okay. I admit it. I looked.

Fat lot of good it did me, too. After he'd collected the test, Mr. Gianini went over the problems on the board, and I got every single one of them wrong anyway.

I CAN'T EVEN CHEAT RIGHT!!!

I have got to be the most pathetic human being on the planet.

polynomials

term: variables multiplied by a coefficient

degree of polynomial = the degree of the term with the
    highest degree

Hello? Does ANYONE care??? I mean, really, truly care about polynomials? I mean, besides people like Michael Moscovitz and Mr. Gianini. Anyone? Anyone at all?

When the bell finally rang, Mr. Gianini goes, "Mia, will I have the pleasure of your company this afternoon at the review session?"

I said yes, but I didn't say it loud enough for anyone to hear but him.

Why me? *Why, why, why?* Like I don't have enough to worry about. I'm flunking Algebra, my mom's dating my teacher, and I'm the princess of Genovia.

Something has just *got* to give.

Tuesday, October 7

Ode to Algebra

Thrust into this dingy classroom
we die like lampless moths
locked into the desolation of
fluorescent lights and metal desks.
Ten minutes until the bell rings.
What use is the quadratic formula
in our daily lives?
Can we use it to unlock the secrets
in the hearts of those we love?
Five minutes until the bell rings.
Cruel Algebra teacher,
won't you let us go?

HOMEWORK

Algebra: problems 17–30 on handout
English: proposal
World Civ: questions at end of Chapter 7
G&T: none
French: *huit* phrase, ex. A, pg. 31
Biology: worksheet

Oh no.

She's here.

Well, not *here*, exactly. But she's in this country. She's in the city. She's only like fifty-seven blocks away, as a matter of fact. She's staying at the Plaza, with Dad. Thank God. Now I'll only have to see her after school and on the weekends. It would suck so bad if she were staying here.

It's pretty awful, seeing her first thing in the morning. She wears these really fancy negligees to bed, with big lace sections that everything shows through. You know. Stuff you wouldn't want to see. Plus, even though she takes her makeup off to sleep, she still has on eyeliner, because she had it tattooed onto her eyelids back in the eighties when she went through a brief manic phase shortly after Princess Grace died (according to my mom). It looks pretty weird, seeing this little old lady in a lace nightie with big black lines around her eyes first thing in the morning.

Actually, it's scary. Scarier than Freddy Kruger and Jason put together.

No wonder Grandpère died of a heart attack in bed. He probably rolled over one morning and got a real good look at his wife.

Somebody ought to warn the president she's here. I mean it; he really ought to know. Because if anybody could start World War III, it's my grandmother.

Last time I saw Grandmère, she was having this dinner party, and she served everybody foie gras except this one woman. She just had Marie, her cook, leave that lady's plate bare for the foie gras course. And when I tried to give the lady my foie gras, because I thought maybe they had run out—and anyway, I don't eat anything that once was alive—my grandmother was all, "Amelia!" She said it so loud, she scared me. She made me drop my slice of foie gras on the floor. Her horrible miniature poodle pried it up off the parquet before I could even move.

And then later, after everybody left, when I asked her why she wouldn't give that lady any foie gras, Grandmère said it was because the lady had had a child out of wedlock.

Hello? Grandmère, may I point out that your own son had a child out of wedlock, namely me, Mia, *your granddaughter?*

But when I said that, Grandmère just yelled for her maid to bring her another drink. Oh, so I guess it's okay to have a child out of wedlock if you're a PRINCE. But if you're just a regular person, no foie gras for you.

Oh, no! What if Grandmère comes to the loft? She's never seen the loft before. I don't think she's ever been below Fifty-seventh Street. She's going to hate it here in the Village, I'm telling you right now. People of the same sex kiss and hold hands in our neighborhood all the time. Grandmère has a fit when she sees people of the *opposite* sex holding hands. What's she going to do during the Gay Pride Parade, when everybody is kissing and holding hands and shouting "We're Here, We're Queer, Get Over It?" Grandmère won't get over it. She might have a heart attack. She doesn't even like pierced ears, let alone pierced anything else.

Plus it's against the law to smoke in restaurants here, and Grandmère smokes all the time, even in bed, which is why Grandpère had these weird disposable oxygen masks installed in every single room at Miragnac and had an underground tunnel dug that we could run through in case Grandmère fell asleep with a cigarette in her mouth and the chateau burst into flames.

Also, Grandmère hates cats. She thinks they jump on children while they're sleeping on purpose to suck out their breath. What's she going to say when she sees Fat Louie? He sleeps in bed with me every night. If he ever jumped on my face, he'd kill me instantly. He weighs twenty-five pounds and seven ounces, and that's before he's had his can of Fancy Feast in the morning.

And can you imagine what she'll do when she sees my mom's collection of wooden fertility goddesses?

Why did she have to come NOW? She's going to ruin EVERYTHING. There's no way I'm going to be able to keep this a secret from everyone with HER around.

Why?

Why??

WHY???

Thursday, October 9

I found out why.
She's giving me princess lessons.
In too much shock to write. More later.

Princess lessons.

I am not kidding. I have to go straight from my Algebra review session every day to princess lessons at the Plaza with my grandmother.

Okay, so if there's a God, how could this have happened?

I mean it. Like, people always talk about how God doesn't ever give you more than you can handle, but I'm telling you right now, I cannot handle this. This is just *too much*! I *cannot* go to princess lessons every day after school. Not with Grandmère. I am seriously considering running away from home.

My dad says I have no choice. Last night, after I left Grandmère's room at the Plaza, I went straight down to his. I banged on the door, and when he answered it I stalked straight in and told him I wasn't doing it. No way. Nobody had told me anything about princess lessons.

And do you know what he said? He says I signed the compromise, so I am obligated to attend princess lessons as part of my duties as his heir.

I said then we are just going to have to revise the compromise, because there was nothing in there about me having to meet with Grandmère every day after school for any princess lessons.

But my dad wouldn't even talk to me about it. He

said he was late and could we please talk about it later. And then while I was standing there, going on about how unfair this all was, in walks this reporter from ABC. I guess she was there to interview him, but it was kind of funny, because I've seen her interview people before, and normally she doesn't wear black sleeveless cocktail dresses when she's interviewing the president or somebody like that.

I'm going to have to take a good look at that compromise tonight, because I don't recall it saying anything about princess lessons.

Here is how my first "lesson" went, yesterday after school:

First the doorman won't even let me in (big surprise). Then he sees Lars, who is like six foot seven and must weigh three hundred pounds. Plus, Lars has this bulge sticking out of his jacket, and I only just now figured out that it's a gun and not the stump of an extraneous third arm, which is what originally I thought. I was too embarrassed to ask him about it, in case it dredged up painful memories for him of being teased as a child in Amsterdam, or wherever he is from. I mean, I know what it's like to be a freak: It's just better not to bring that kind of thing up.

But no, it's a gun, and the doorman got all upset about it and called the concierge over. Thank God the concierge recognized Lars, who's staying there, after all, in a room in Dad's suite.

So then the concierge himself escorted me upstairs to the penthouse, which is where Grandmère is staying. Let me tell you about this penthouse: It is very fancy. I thought the ladies' room at the Plaza was fancy? The ladies' room is nothing compared to this penthouse.

First of all, everything is pink. Pink walls, pink carpet, pink curtains, pink furniture. There are pink roses everywhere, and these portraits hanging on the walls that all feature pink-cheeked shepherdesses and stuff.

And just when I thought I was going to drown in pinkness, out came Grandmère, dressed completely in purple, from her silk turban all the way down to her mules with the rhinestone clips on the toes.

At least, I think they're rhinestones.

Grandmère always wears purple. Lilly says people who wear purple a lot usually have borderline personality disorders, because they have delusions of grandeur. Traditionally, purple has always stood for the aristocracy, since for hundreds of years peasants weren't allowed to dye their clothes with indigo, and therefore couldn't make violet.

Of course, Lilly doesn't know my grandmother IS a member of the aristocracy. So while Grandmère is definitely delusional, it's not because she THINKS she's an aristocrat; she really IS one.

So Grandmère comes in off the terrace, where she was standing, and the first thing she says to me is,

"What's that writing on your shoe?"

But I didn't need to worry about getting caught cheating, because Grandmère started in right away about everything else that was wrong with me.

"Why are you wearing tennis shoes with a skirt? Are those tights supposed to be clean? Why can't you stand up straight? What's wrong with your hair? Have you been biting your nails again, Amelia? I thought we agreed you were going to give up that nasty habit. My God, can't you stop growing? Is it your goal to be as tall as your father?"

Only it sounded even worse, because it was all in French.

And then, as if that wasn't bad enough, she goes, in her creaky old cigaretty voice, "Haven't you a kiss for your *grandmère*, then?"

So I go up to her and bend down (my grandmother is like a foot shorter than me) and kiss her on the cheek (which is very soft because she rubs Vaseline on her face every night before she goes to bed), and then when I start to pull away she grabs me and goes, "*Pfui!* Have you forgotten *everything* I taught you?" and makes me kiss her on the other cheek, too, because in Europe (and SoHo), that's how you say hello to people.

Anyway, I bent down and kissed Grandmère on the other cheek, and as I did so I noticed Rommel peeking out from behind her. Rommel is Grandmère's fifteen-year-old miniature poodle. He is the same shape and size as an iguana, only not as smart. He shakes all the time and has to wear a fleece jacket. Today his jacket was the same purple as Grandmère's dress. Rommel won't let anyone touch him except for Grandmère, and even then he rolls his eyes around as if he were being tortured while she's petting him.

If Noah had ever met Rommel, he might have changed his mind about letting two of *all* of God's creatures on the ark.

"Now," Grandmère said when she felt we'd been affectionate enough, "let's see if I have this right: Your father tells you that you are the princess of Genovia and you burst into tears. Why is this?"

All of a sudden, I got very tired. I had to sit down on one of the pink foofy chairs before I fell down.

"Oh, Grandmère," I said in English. "I don't want to be a princess. I just want to be me, Mia."

Grandmère said, "Don't converse in English with me. It's vulgar. Speak French when you speak to me. Sit up straight in that chair. Do not drape your legs over the arm. And you are not Mia. You are Amelia. In fact, you are Amelia Mignonette Grimaldi Renaldo."

I said, "You forgot Thermopolis," and Grandmère gave me the evil eye. She is very good at this.

"No," she said. "I did not forget Thermopolis."

Then Grandmère sat down in the foofy chair next to mine and said, "Are you telling me you have no wish to assume your rightful place upon the throne?"

Boy, was I tired. "Grandmère, you know as well as I do that I'm not princess material, okay? So why are we even wasting our time?"

Grandmère looked at me out of her twin tattoos of eyeliner. I could tell she wanted to kill me but probably couldn't figure out how to do it without getting blood on the pink carpet.

"You are the heir to the crown of Genovia," she said in this totally serious voice. "And you will take my son's place on the throne when he dies. This is how it is. There is no other way."

Oh, boy.

So I kind of went, "Yeah, whatever, Grandmère. Look, I got a lot of homework. Is this princess thing going to take long?"

Grandmère just looked at me. "It will take," she said, "as long as it takes. I am not afraid to sacrifice my time—or even myself—for the good of my country."

Whoa. This was getting way patriotic. "Um," I said. "Okay."

So then I stared at Grandmère for a while, and she stared back at me, and Rommel laid down on the carpet between our chairs, only he did it really slow, like his legs were too delicate to support all two pounds of him, and then Grandmère broke the silence by saying, "We will begin tomorrow. You will come here directly after school."

"Um, Grandmère. I can't come here directly after

school. I'm flunking Algebra. I have to go to a review session every day after school."

"Then after that. No dawdling. You will bring with you a list of the ten women you admire most in the world, and why. That is all."

My mouth fell open. *Homework?* There's going to be *homework?* Nobody said anything about homework!

"And close your mouth," she barked. "It is uncouth to let it hang open like that."

I closed my mouth. Homework???

"Tomorrow you will wear nylons. Not tights. Not kneesocks. You are too old for tights and kneesocks. And you will wear your school shoes, not tennis sneakers. You will style your hair, apply lipstick, and paint your fingernails—what's left of them, anyway." Grandmère stood up. She didn't even have to push up with her hands on the arms of her chair, either. Grandmère's pretty spry for her age. "Now I must dress for dinner with the shah. Good-bye."

I just sat there. Was she insane? Was she completely nuts? Did she have the slightest idea what she was asking me to do?

Evidently she did, since the next thing I knew Lars was standing there, and Grandmère and Rommel were gone.

Geez! Homework!!! Nobody said there was going to be homework.

And that's not the worst of it. Panty hose? To school? I mean, the only girls who wear panty hose to school are girls like Lana Weinberger, and seniors, and people like that. You know. Show-offs. None of *my* friends wear panty hose.

And, I might add, none of my friends wear lipstick or nail polish or do their hair. Not for *school*, anyway.

But what choice did I have? Grandmère totally scared me, with her tattooed eyelids and all. I couldn't NOT do what she said.

So what I did was, I borrowed a pair of my mom's panty hose. She wears them whenever she has an open-ing—and on dates with Mr. Gianini, I've noticed. I took a pair of her panty hose to school with me in my back-pack. I didn't have any fingernails to paint—according to Lilly, I am orally fixated; if it fits in my mouth, I'll put it there—but I did borrow one of my mom's lipsticks, too. And I tried some mousse I found in the medicine cabinet. It must have worked, since when Lilly got into the car this morning, she said, "Wow. Where'd you pick up the Jersey girl, Lars?"

Which I guess meant that my hair looked really big, like girls from New Jersey wear it when they come into Manhattan for a romantic dinner in Little Italy with their boyfriends.

So then, after my review session with Mr. G at the end of the day, I went into the girls' room and put on the panty hose, the lipstick, and my loafers, which are too small and pinch my toes really bad. When I checked myself out in the mirror, I thought I didn't look so bad.

I didn't think Grandmère would have any complaints.

I thought I was pretty slick, waiting to change until after school. I figured on a Friday afternoon there wouldn't be anyone hanging around. Who wants to hang around school on a Friday?

I had forgotten, of course, about the Computer Club.

Everybody forgets about the Computer Club, even the people who belong to it. They don't have any friends, except each other, and they never go on dates— only unlike me, I think this is by choice: No one at Albert Einstein is smart enough for them—except, again, for each other.

Anyway, I walked out of the girls' room and ran smack into Lilly's brother, Michael. He's the Computer Club treasurer. He's smart enough to be president, but he says he has no interest in being a fig-urehead.

"Christ, Thermopolis," he said, as I scrambled around, trying to pick up all the stuff I'd dropped—like my high-tops and socks and stuff—when I bumped into him. "What happened to *you*?"

I thought he meant why was I there so late. "You know I have to meet with Mr. Gianini every day after school because I'm flunking Alge—"

"I know *that*." Michael held up the lipstick that had exploded out of my backpack. "I mean what's with the war paint?"

I took it away from him. "Nothing. Don't tell Lilly."

"Don't tell Lilly what?" I stood up, and he noticed the panty hose. "Jesus, Thermopolis. Where are *you* going?"

"Nowhere." Must I continuously be forced to lie all the time? I really wished he would go away. Plus a bunch of his computer nerd friends were standing there, staring at me like I was some new kind of pixel or something. It was making me pretty uncomfortable.

"Nobody goes *nowhere* looking like that." Michael shifted his laptop from one arm to the other, then got this funny look on his face. "Thermopolis, are you going out on a *date?*"

"*What?* No, I'm not going on a date!" I was completely shocked at the idea. A *date? Me?* I'm so sure! "I have to meet my grandmother!"

Michael didn't look as if he believed me. "And do you usually wear lipstick and panty hose to meet your grandmother?"

I heard some discreet coughing, and looked down the hall. Lars was there by the doors, waiting for me.

I guess I could have stood there and explained that my grandmother had threatened me with bodily harm (well, practically) if I didn't wear makeup and nylons to meet her. But I sort of didn't think he'd believe me. So I said, "Look, don't tell Lilly, okay?"

Then I ran away.

I knew I was dead meat. There was no way Michael

wasn't going to tell his sister about seeing me coming out of the girls' room after school in lipstick and panty hose. No way.

And Grandmère's was HORRIBLE. She said the lipstick I had on made me look like a *poulet*. At least that's what I thought she said, and I couldn't figure out why she thought I looked like a chicken. But just now I looked up *poulet* in my English-French dictionary, and it turns out *poulet* can also mean "prostitute"! My grandmother called me a hooker!

Geez! Whatever happened to nice grandmothers, who bake brownies for you and tell you how precious you are? It's just my luck I get one who has tattooed eyeliner and tells me *I* look like a hooker.

And she said that the panty hose I had on were the wrong color. How could they be the wrong color? They're panty hose color! Then she made me practice sitting down so my underwear didn't show between my legs for like two hours!

I'm thinking about calling Amnesty International. This has to constitute torture.

And when I gave her my essay on the ten women I admire most, she read it and then ripped it up into little pieces! I am not even kidding!

I couldn't help screaming, "Grandmère, why'd you do that?" and she went, all calmly, "These are not the sort of women you should be admiring. You should be admiring *real* women."

I asked Grandmère what she meant by "*real women,*" because all of the women on my list are real. I mean, Madonna might have had a little plastic surgery, but she's still *real.*

But Grandmère says real women are Princess Grace and Coco Chanel. I pointed out to her that Princess Diana is on my list, and you know what she said? She says she thinks Princess Diana was a "twink"! That's what she called her. A "twink."

Only she pronounced it "tweenk."

Geez!

After we'd rehearsed sitting for an hour, Grandmère said she had to go and take a bath, since she's having dinner tonight with some prime minister. She told me to be at the Plaza tomorrow no later than ten o'clock—A.M. 10 A.M.!

"Grandmère," I said. "Tomorrow is Saturday."

"I know it."

"But Grandmère," I said. "Saturdays are when I help my friend Lilly film her TV show—"

But Grandmère asked me which was more important, Lilly's TV show or the well-being of the people of Genovia, who, in case you didn't know, number in the 50,000 range.

I guess 50,000 people are more important than one episode of *Lilly Tells It Like It Is.* Still, it's going to be tough explaining to Lilly why I won't be there to hold the camera when she confronts Mr. and Mrs. Ho, owners of Ho's Deli, across the street from Albert Einstein, about their unfair pricing policies. Lilly has discovered that Mr. and Mrs. Ho give significant discounts to the Asian students who go to Albert Einstein, but no discounts at all to the Caucasian, African American, Latino, or Arab students. Lilly discovered this yesterday after play rehearsal when she went to buy ginkgo biloba puffs and Ling Su, in front of her in line, bought the same thing. But Mrs. Ho charged her (Lilly) *five whole cents more* than Ling Su for the same product.

And then when Lilly complained, Mrs. Ho pretended like she couldn't speak English, even though she must speak some English, or why else would her mini-TV behind the counter always be tuned to Judge Judy?

Lilly has decided to secretly videotape the Hos to gather evidence of their blatantly preferential treatment of Asian Americans. She's calling for a school-wide boycott of Ho's Deli.

The thing is, I think Lilly's making a really big deal about five cents. But Lilly says it's the principle of the thing, and that maybe if people had made a big deal about how the Nazis smashed up Jewish people's store windows on Kristalnacht they wouldn't have ended up putting so many people in ovens.

I don't know. The Hos aren't exactly Nazis. They're very nice to the little cat they've raised from a kitten to chase rats away from the chicken wings in the salad bar.

Maybe I'm not too sorry about missing the taping tomorrow.

But I *am* sorry Grandmère tore up my list of the ten women I admire most. I thought it was *nice*. When I got home, I printed it out again, just because it made me so mad, her tearing it up like that. I put a copy in this book.

And after carefully reviewing my copy of the Thermopolis-Renaldo Compromise, I see *nothing* about princess lessons. Something is going to have to be done about this. I have been leaving messages for Dad all night, but he doesn't answer. Where *is* he?

Lilly isn't home, either. Maya says the Moscovitzes went to Great Shanghai for dinner as a family, in order to grow to understand one another better as human beings.

I wish Lilly would hurry up and get home and call me back. I don't want her to think I'm in any way against her groundbreaking investigation into Ho's Deli. I just want to tell her the reason I won't be able to be there is because I have to spend the day with my grandmother.

I hate my life.

THE TEN WOMEN I ADMIRE MOST
IN THE WHOLE WORLD
by Mia Thermopolis

Madonna. Madonna Ciccone revolutionized the fashion world with her iconoclastic sense of style, sometimes offending people who are not very open-minded—for instance, her rhinestone cross earrings, which made many Christian groups ban her CDs—or who have no sense of humor—like Pepsi, which didn't like it when she danced in front of some burning crosses. It was because she wasn't afraid to make people like the Pope mad that Madonna became one of the richest female entertainers in the world, paving the way for women performers everywhere by showing them that it is possible to be sexy onstage and smart off it.

Princess Diana. Even though she is dead, Princess Diana is one of my favorite women of all time. She, too, revolutionized the fashion world by refusing to wear the ugly old hats that her mother-in-law told her to wear, and instead wore Halston and Bill Blass. Also she visited a lot of really sick people, even though nobody made her do it, and some people, like her husband, even made fun of her for doing it. The night Princess Diana died I unplugged the TV and said I would never watch it again, since media was what killed her. But then I regretted it the next morning when I couldn't watch Japanese anime on the Sci-Fi channel, because unplugging the TV scrambled our cable box.

Hillary Rodham Clinton. Hillary Rodham Clinton totally recognized that her thick ankles were detracting from her image as a serious politician, and so she started wearing pants. Also, even though everybody was talking bad about her all the time for not leaving her husband, who was going around having sex with people behind her back, she pretended like nothing was going on and went on running the country, just like she'd always done, which is how a president should behave.

Picabo Street. She won all those gold medals in skiing, all because she just practiced like crazy and never gave up, even when she was crashing into fences and things. Plus she picked her own name, which is cool.

Leola Mae Harmon. I saw a movie about her on the Lifetime channel. Leola was an air force nurse who was in a car accident and the lower part of her face got all mangled, but then Armand Assante, who plays a plastic surgeon, said he could fix her. Leola had to endure hours of painful reconstructive surgery, during which her husband left her because she didn't have any lips (which I guess is why the movie is called *Why Me?*). Armand Assante said he would make her a new pair of lips, only the other air force doctors didn't like the fact that he wanted to make them out of skin from Leola's vagina. But he did it anyway, and then he and Leola got married and worked together to help give other accident victims vagina lips. And the whole thing turned out to have been *based on a true story.*

Joan of Arc. Joan of Arc—or Jeanne d'Arc as they say in France—lived in like the twelfth century and one day when she was my age she heard this angel's voice tell her to take up arms and go help the French army fight against the British (the French were always fighting the British, all the way up until the Nazis attacked, and then they were like, "*Zut alors!* Can you help us?" and the British had to go in and try to save their lazy butts, for which nobody French has ever been properly grateful, as exemplified by their sloppy highway maintenance; see death of Princess Diana, above). Anyway, Joan cut off her hair and got herself a suit of armor, just like Mulan in the Disney movie, and went and led the French forces to victory in a number of battles. But then, like typical politicians, the French government decided Joan was too powerful, so they accused her of being a witch and burned her to death at the stake. And unlike Lilly, I do NOT believe that Joan was suffering from adolescent onset schizophrenia. I think angels really DID talk to her. None of the schizophrenics in our school have ever had their voices tell them to do something cool like lead their country into battle. All Brandon Hertzenbaum's voices told him to do was go into the boys' room and carve "Satan" in the door to the bathroom stall with a protractor. So there you go.

Christy. Christy is not really a person. She is the fictional heroine of my favorite book of all time, which is called *Christy*, by Catherine Marshall. Christy is a young girl who goes to teach school in the Smokey Mountains at the turn of the century because she believes she can make a difference, and all these really hot guys fall in love with her and she learns about God and typhoid and stuff. Only I can't tell anyone, especially Lilly, that this is my favorite book, because it's kind of sappy and religious, and plus it doesn't have any spaceships or serial killers in it.

The Lady Cop I Once Saw give a truck driver a ticket for honking at a woman who was crossing the street (her skirt was kind of short). The lady cop told the truck driver it was a no-honking zone, and then when he argued about it, she wrote him another ticket for arguing with an officer of the law.

Lilly Moscovitz. Lilly Moscovitz isn't really a woman, yet, but she's someone I admire very much. She is very, very smart, but unlike many very smart people, she doesn't rub it in all the time, the fact that she's so much smarter than me. Well, at least, not much. Lilly is always thinking up fun things for us to do, like go to Barnes & Noble and secretly film me asking Dr. Laura, who was signing books there, if she knows so much how come she's divorced, then showing it on her (Lilly's) TV show, including the part where we got thrown out and banned from the Union Square Barnes & Noble forever after. Lilly is my best friend and I tell her everything, except the part about me being a princess, which I don't think she'd understand.

Helen Thermopolis. Helen Thermopolis, besides being my mother, is a very talented artist who was recently featured in *Art in America* magazine as one of the most important painters of the new millennium. Her painting *Woman Waiting for Price Check at the Grand Union* won this big national award and sold for $140,000, only part of which my mom got to keep, since 15 percent of it went to her gallery and half of what was left went to taxes, which sucks, if you ask me. But even though she's such an important artist, my mom always has time for me. I also respect her because she is deeply principled: She says she would never think of inflicting her beliefs on others and would thank others to pay her the same courtesy.

Can you believe Grandmère tore this up? I'm telling you, this is the sort of essay that could bring a country to its knees.

So I was right: Lilly *does* think the reason I'm not participating in the taping today is because I'm against her boycott of the Hos.

I told her that wasn't true, that I had to spend the day with my grandmother. But guess what? She doesn't believe me. The one time I tell the truth, and she doesn't believe me!

Lilly says that if I really wanted to get out of spending the day with Grandmère I could, but because I'm so codependent, I can't say no to anyone. Which doesn't even make sense, since obviously I am saying no to *her*. When I pointed that out to Lilly, though, she just got madder. I can't say no to my grandmother, since she's like sixty-five years old, and she's going to die soon, if there's any justice at all in the world.

Besides, you don't know my grandmother, I said. You don't say no to my grandmother.

Then Lilly went, "No, I don't know your grandmother, do I, Mia? Isn't that curious, considering the fact that you know all *my* grandparents"—the Moscovitzes have me over every year for Passover dinner—"and yet I haven't met any of *yours*?"

Well, of course the reason for *that* is that my mom's parents are like total farmers who live in a place called Versailles, Indiana, only they pronounce it "Ver-sales." My mom's parents are *afraid* to come to New York City because they say there are too many "furinners"—by which they mean foreigners—here, and anything that isn't 100 percent American scares them, which is one of the reasons my mom left home when she was eighteen and has only been back twice, and that was with me. Let me tell you, Versailles is a small, small town. It's so small that there's a sign on the door at the bank that says IF BANK IS CLOSED, PLEASE SLIDE MONEY UNDER DOOR. I am not lying, either. I took a photo of it and brought it back to show everyone because I knew they wouldn't believe me. It's hanging on our refrigerator.

Anyway, Grandpa and Grandma Thermopolis don't make it out of Indiana much.

And the reason I'd never introduced Lilly to Grandmère Renaldo is because Grandmère Renaldo hates children. And I can't introduce her now because then Lilly will find out I'm the princess of Genovia, and you can bet I'll never hear the end of *that*. She'd probably want to interview me, or something, for her TV show. That's all I need: My name and image plastered all over Manhattan Public Access.

So I was telling Lilly all of this—about how I had to go out with my grandmother, not about my being a princess, of course—and as I was talking I could hear her breathing over the phone in that way she does when she's mad, and finally she just goes, "Oh, come over tonight then, and help me edit," and slammed the phone down.

Geez.

Well, at least Michael didn't tell her about the lipstick and panty hose. *That* would have really made her mad. She never would have believed I was only going to my grandmother's. No way.

This was all at like nine-thirty, while I was getting ready to go to Grandmère's. Grandmère told me that for today I don't have to wear lipstick or panty hose. She said I could wear anything I wanted. So I wore my overalls. I know she hates them, but hey, she said anything I wanted. Hee hee hee.

Oops, gotta go. Lars just pulled up in front of the Plaza. We're here.

I can never go to school again. I can never go *any-where* again. I will never leave this loft, ever, ever again.

You won't believe what she did to me. *I* can't believe what she did to me. I can't believe my dad *let* her do this to me.

Well, he's going to pay. He's totally paying for this, and I mean BIG. As soon as I got home (right after my mom went, "Well, hey, Rosemary. Where's your baby?" which I suppose was some kind of joke about my new haircut, but it was NOT funny), I marched right up to him and said, "You are paying for this. Big time."

Who says I have a fear of confrontation?

He totally tried to get out of it, going, "What do you mean? Mia, I think you look beautiful. Don't listen to your mother, what does she know? I like your hair. It's so . . . short."

Gee, I wonder why? Maybe because his mother met Lars and me in the lobby as soon as we'd turned the car over to the valet, and just pointed at the door. Just pointed at the door again, and said, "*On y va,*" which in English means "Let's go."

"Let's go where?" I asked, all innocently (this was this morning, remember, back when I was still innocent).

"Chez Paolo," Grandmère said. *Chez Paolo* means "Paul's house." So I thought we were going to meet one of her friends, maybe for brunch or something, and I thought, huh, cool, field trip. Maybe these princess lessons won't be so bad.

But then we got there, and I saw Chez Paolo wasn't a house at all. At first I couldn't tell what it was. It looked a little like a really fancy hospital—it was all frosted glass and these Japanese-looking trees. And then we got inside; all of these skinny young people were floating around, dressed all in black. They were all excited to see my grandmother, and took us to this little room where there were these couches and all these magazines. So then I figured Grandmère maybe had some plastic surgery scheduled, and while I am sort of against plastic surgery—unless you're like Leola Mae and you need lips—I was like, Well, at least she'll be off my back for a while.

Boy, was I ever wrong! Paolo isn't a doctor. I doubt he's ever even been to college! Paolo is a *stylist*! Worse, he styles *people*! I'm serious. He takes unfashionable, frumpy people like me, and he makes them stylish—for a *living*. And Grandmère sicced him on *me*! *Me!!* Like it's bad enough I don't have breasts. She has to tell some guy named *Paolo* that?

What kind of name is Paolo, anyway? I mean, this is America, for Pete's sake! YOUR NAME IS PAUL!!!

That's what I wanted to scream at him. But, of course, I couldn't. I mean, it wasn't Paolo's fault my grandmother dragged me there. And as he pointed out to me, he only made time for me in his incredibly busy schedule because Grandmère told him it was this big emergency.

God, how embarrassing. *I'm* a fashion emergency.

Anyway, I was plenty peeved at Grandmère, but I couldn't start yelling at her right there in front of Paolo. She totally knew it, too. She just sat there on this velvet couch, petting Rommel, who was sitting on her lap with his legs crossed—she's even taught her *dog* to sit lady-like, and *he's* a boy—sipping a Sidecar she got some-body to make for her and reading *W*.

Meanwhile, Paolo was picking up chunks of my hair and making this face and going, all sadly, "It must go. It must *all* go."

And it went. All of it. Well, almost all of it. I still have some like bangs and a little fringe in back.

Did I mention that I'm no longer a dishwater blond? No. I'm just a plain old blond now.

And Paolo didn't stop there. Oh, no. I now have fin-gernails. I am not kidding. For the first time in my life, I have fingernails. They're completely fake, but I have them. And it looks like I'll have them for a while: I already tried to pull one off, and it HURT. What kind of secret astronaut glue did that manicurist use, anyway?

You might be wondering why, if I didn't want to have all my hair cut off and fake fingernails glued over my real, stumpy fingernails, I let them do all that.

I'm sort of wondering that myself. I mean, I know I have a fear of confrontation. So it wasn't like I was going to throw down my glass of lemonade and say, "Okay, stop making a fuss over me, right now!" I mean, they gave me lemonade! Can you imagine that? At the International House of Hair, which is where my mom and I usually go, over on Sixth Avenue, they sure don't give you lemonade, but it *does* only cost $9.99 for a cut and blow dry.

And it is sort of hard when all these beautiful, fashionable people are telling you how good you'd look in *this* and how much *that* would bring out your cheekbones, to remember you're a feminist and an environmentalist, and don't believe in using makeup or chemicals that might be harmful to the earth. I mean, I didn't want to hurt their feelings, or cause a scene, or anything like that.

And I kept telling myself, She's only doing this because she loves you. My grandmother, I mean. I know she probably wasn't doing it for that reason—I don't think Grandmère loves me any more than I love her—but I *told* myself that, anyway.

I told myself that after we left Paolo's and went to Bergdorf Goodman, where Grandmère bought me four pairs of shoes that cost almost as much as the removal of that sock from Fat Louie's small intestines. I told myself that after she bought me a bunch of clothes I will never wear. I did tell her I would never wear these

clothes, but she just waved at me. Like, Go on, go on.
You tell such amusing stories.

Well, I for one will not stand for it. There isn't a
single inch of me that hasn't been pinched, cut, filed,
painted, sloughed, blown dry, or moisturized. I even
have fingernails.

But I am not happy. I am not a bit happy.
Grandmère's happy. *Grandmère's* head over heels happy
about how I look. Because I don't look a thing like Mia
Thermopolis. Mia Thermopolis never had fingernails.
Mia Thermopolis never had blond highlights. Mia
Thermopolis never wore makeup or Gucci shoes or
Chanel skirts or Christian Dior bras, which, by the way,
don't even come in 32A, which is my size. I don't even
know who I am anymore. It certainly isn't Mia
Thermopolis.

She's turning me into someone else.

So I stood in front of my father, looking like a human
Q-tip in my new hair, and I let him have it.

"First she makes me do homework. Then she rips the
homework up. Then she gives me sitting lessons. Then
she has all my hair dyed a different color and most of it
hacked off, makes someone glue tiny surfboards to my fingernails, buys me shoes that cost as much as small animal
surgery, and clothes that make me look like Vicky, the
captain's daughter in that old seventies series *The Love
Boat.*

"Well, Dad, I'm sorry, but I'm not Vicky, and I never

will be, no matter how much Grandmère dresses me up like her. I'm not going to do great in school, be super-cheerful all the time, or have any shipboard romances. That's Vicky. That's not me!"

My mom was coming out of her bedroom, putting the last touches on her date wear, when I screamed this. She was wearing a new outfit. It was this sort of Spanish skirt in all these different colors, and a sort of off-the-shoulder top. Her long hair was all over the place, and she looked really great. In fact, my dad headed for the liquor cabinet again when he saw her.

"Mia," my mom said as she fastened on an earring, "nobody is asking you to be Vicky, the captain's daughter."

"Grandmère is!"

"Your grandmother is just trying to prepare you, Mia."

"Prepare me for what? I can't go to school looking like this, you know," I yelled.

My mom looked kind of confused. "Why not?"

Oh my God. Why me?

"Because," I said, as patiently as I could, "I don't want anyone at school finding out I'm the princess of Genovia!"

My mom shook her head. "Mia, honey, they're going to find out sometime."

I don't see how. See, I have it all worked out: I'll only be a princess in Genovia, and since the chances of any-body I know from school ever actually going to Genovia are like none, no one here will ever find out, so I'm totally safe from being branded a freak, like Tina Hakim Baba. Well, at least not the kind of freak who has to ride in a chauffeured limo to school every day and be followed by bodyguards.

"Well," my mom said, after I'd told her all this. "What if it's in the newspaper?"

"Why would it be in the newspaper?"

My mom looked at my dad. My dad looked away and took a sip from his drink.

You wouldn't believe what he did next. He put down his drink, then he reached into his pants pocket, took out his Prada wallet, opened it, and asked, "How much?"

I was shocked. So was my mom.

"Phillipe," she said, but my dad just kept looking at me.

"I'm serious, Helen," he said. "I can see the compromise we drew up is getting us nowhere. The only solution in matters like these is cold, hard cash. So how much do I have to pay you, Mia, to let your grandmother turn you into a princess?"

"Is that what she's doing?" I started yelling some more. "Well, if that's what she's doing, she has it all screwed up. I never saw a princess with hair this short, or feet as big as mine, who didn't have breasts!"

My dad just looked at his watch. I guess he had somewhere to go. I bet it was another "interview" with

131

that blond anchorwoman from ABC News.

"Consider it a job," he said, "this learning how to be a princess business. I will pay your salary. Now, how much do you want?"

I started yelling even more about personal integrity and how I refused to sell my soul to the company store, that kind of thing. Stuff I got from some of my mom's old records. I think she recognized this, since she sort of started slinking away, saying she had to go get ready for her date with Mr. G. My dad shot her the evil eye— he can do it almost as well as Grandmère—and then he sighed and went, "Mia, I will donate one hundred dollars a day, in your name, to—what is it? Oh, yes— Greenpeace, so they can save all the whales they want, if you will make my mother happy by letting her teach you to be a princess."

Well.

That's an entirely different matter. It would be one thing if he were paying *me* to have my hair color chemically altered. But paying one hundred dollars per day to Greenpeace? That's $356,000 per year! In my name! Why, Greenpeace will *have* to hire me after I graduate. I practically will have donated a million dollars by that time!

Wait, maybe that's only $36,500. Where's my calculator????

Well, I don't know who Lilly Moscovitz thinks she is, but I sure know who she isn't: my friend. I don't think anyone who was my friend would be as mean to me as Lilly was tonight. I couldn't believe it. And all because of my *hair*!

I guess I could understand it if Lilly was mad at me about something that mattered—like missing the taping of the Ho segment. I mean, I'm like the main camera-person for *Lilly Tells It Like It Is*. I also do a lot of the prop work. When I'm not there, Shameeka has to do my job as well as hers, and Shameeka is already executive producer and location scout.

So I guess I could see how Lilly might kind of resent the fact that I missed today's taping. She thinks Ho-Gate—that's what she's calling it—is the most important story she's ever done. I think it's kind of stupid. Who cares about five cents, anyway? But Lilly's all, "We're going to break the cycle of racism that has been rampant in delis across the five boroughs."

Whatever. All I know is, I walked into the Moscovitzes' apartment tonight, and Lilly took one look at my new hair and was like, "Oh my God, what happened to you?"

Like I had frostbite all over my face, and my nose had turned black and fallen off, like those people who climbed Mt. Everest.

Okay, I knew people were going to freak and stuff when they saw my hair. I totally washed it before I came over, and got all the mousse and goop out of it. Plus I took off all the makeup Paolo had slathered on me, and put on my overalls and high-tops (you can hardly see the quadratic formula anymore). I really thought, except for my hair, I looked mostly normal. In fact, I kind of thought maybe I looked good—for me, I mean.

But I guess Lilly didn't think so.

I tried to be casual, like it was no big deal. Which it isn't, by the way. It wasn't as if I'd had breast implants or something.

"Yeah," I said, taking off my coat. "Well, my grandmother made me go see this guy Paolo, and he—"

But Lilly wouldn't even let me finish. She was in this state of shock. She went, "Your hair is the same color as Lana Weinberger's."

"Well," I said. "I know."

"What's on your *fingers*? Are those fake fingernails? Lana has those, too!" She stared at me all bug-eyed. "Oh my God, Mia. You're turning into Lana Weinberger!"

Now, that kind of peeved me off. I mean, in the first place, I am *not* turning into Lana Weinberger. In the second place, even if I am, Lilly's the one who's always going on about how stupid people are for not seeing that it doesn't matter what anybody looks like; what matters is what's going on on the inside.

So I stood there in the Moscovitzes' foyer, which is made out of black marble, with Pavlov jumping up and down against my legs because he was so excited to see me, going, "It wasn't me. It was my grandmother. I had to—"

"What do you mean, you had to?" Lilly got this really crabby look on her face. It was the same look she gets every year when our PE instructor tells us we have to run around the reservoir in Central Park for the Presidential Fitness test. Lilly doesn't like to run anywhere, particularly around the reservoir in Central Park (it's really big).

"What are you?" she wanted to know. "Completely passive? You're mute or something? Unable to say the word *no*? You know, Mia, we really need to work on your assertiveness. You seem to have real issues with your grandmother. I mean, you certainly don't have any trouble saying no to *me*. I could have really used your help today with the Ho segment, and you totally let me down. But you've got no problem letting your grandmother cut off all your hair and dye it yellow—"

Okay, now keep in mind I'd just spent the whole day hearing how bad I looked—at least, until Paolo got ahold of me and made me look like Lana Weinberger. Now I had to hear there was something wrong with my personality, too.

So I cracked. I said, "Lilly, *shut up*."

I have never told Lilly to shut up before. Not ever. I

don't think I have ever told anyone to shut up before. It's just not something I do. I don't know what happened, really. Maybe it was the fingernails. I never had fingernails before. They sort of made me feel strong. I mean, really, why was Lilly *always* telling me what to do?

Unfortunately, right as I was telling Lilly to shut up, Michael came out, holding an empty cereal bowl and not wearing a shirt.

"Whoa," he said, backing up. I wasn't sure if he said whoa and backed up because of what I'd said or how I looked.

"What?" Lilly said. "*What* did you just say to me?" Now she looked more like a pug than *ever*.

I totally wanted to back down. But I didn't, because I knew she was right: I *do* have problems being assertive.

So instead I said, "I'm tired of you putting me down all the time. All day long, my mom and dad and grandmother and teachers are telling me what to do. I don't need my *friends* getting on my case, too."

"Whoa," Michael said again. This time I knew it was because of what I said.

"What," Lilly said, her eyes getting all narrow, "is your *problem*?"

I went, "You know what? I don't have a problem. *You're* the one with the problem. You seem to have a big problem with me. Well, you know what? I'm going to solve your problem for you. I'm leaving. I never wanted to help you with your stupid Ho-Gate story anyway. The Hos are nice people. They haven't done anything wrong. I don't see why you have to pick on them. And"—I said this as I opened the door—"my hair is *not* yellow."

Then I left. I sort of slammed the door behind me, too.

While I was waiting for the elevator, I sort of thought Lilly might come out and apologize to me.

But she didn't.

I came straight home, took a bath, and got into bed with my remote control and Fat Louie, who's the only person who likes me the way I am right now. I was thinking Lilly might call to apologize, but so far she hasn't.

Well, I'm not apologizing until she does.

And you know what? I looked in the mirror a minute ago, and my hair doesn't look that bad.

Past Midnight, Sunday, October 12

She still hasn't called.

Sunday, October 12

Oh my God. I am so embarrassed. I wish I could disappear. You will never believe what just happened.

I walked out of my room to get breakfast, and there were my mom and Mr. Gianini sitting at the table eating pancakes!

And Mr. Gianini was wearing a T-shirt and boxer shorts!! My mom was in her kimono!!! When she saw me, she choked on her orange juice. Then she went, "Mia, what are you doing here? I thought you spent the night at Lilly's."

I wish I had. I wish I had never chosen to be assertive last night. I could have stayed over at the Moscovitzes' and never had to look at Mr. Gianini in his boxer shorts. I could have lived a full and happy life without ever having seen *that*.

Not to mention him seeing me in my bright red flannel nightie.

How am I ever going to go to a review session again?

This is so horrible. I wish I could call Lilly, but I guess we are fighting.

Later on Sunday

Oh, okay. According to my mom, who just came into my room, Mr. Gianini spent the night on the futon couch because a train on the line he normally takes to his apartment in Brooklyn derailed, and it was going to be out of service for hours, so she told him to just stay over.

If I were still friends with Lilly, she would probably say that my mother was lying to compensate for having traumatized my perception of her as a strictly maternal, and therefore nonsexual, being. That's what Lilly always says when anybody's mother has a guy over and then lies about it.

I prefer to believe my mom's lie, though. The only way I will ever pass Algebra is to believe my mother's lie, because I could never sit there and concentrate on polynomials knowing that the guy in front of me has not only probably stuck his tongue in my mom's mouth but also probably seen her naked.

Why do all these bad things keep happening to me? I would think it would be time for something good to happen to me for a change.

After my mom came in and lied to me, I got dressed and went out into the kitchen to make breakfast. I had to, because my mom wouldn't bring me breakfast in my room, like I asked her. Actually, she went, "Who do you think you are, anyway? The princess of Genovia?"

Which I suppose she thinks is hysterically funny, but really it isn't.

By the time I left my room, Mr. Gianini had gotten dressed, too. He was trying to be all jokey about what had happened, which is the only way you can be about it, I guess.

I wasn't feeling too jokey at first. But then Mr. G started talking about what it would be like to see certain people from Albert Einstein in their pajamas. Like Principal Gupta. Mr. G thinks Principal Gupta probably wears a football jersey to bed, with her husband's sweat pants. I kind of started to laugh, thinking about Principal Gupta in sweatpants. I said I bet Mrs. Hill wears a negligee, one of those fancy ones with the feathers and stuff. But Mr. G said he thought Mrs. Hill was more into flannel than feathers. I wonder how Mr. G knows. Did he go out with Mrs. Hill, too? For a boring guy with so many pens in his shirt pocket, he sure gets around.

After breakfast, my mom and Mr. Gianini tried to get me to go to Central Park with them, because it was all nice outside and everything, but I said I had too much homework, which wasn't too big of a lie. I *do* have homework—Mr. G should know—but not that much. I just didn't really want to be hanging around with a couple. It's like when Shameeka started going with Aaron Ben-Simon in the seventh grade, and she wanted us to go with her to the movies with him and stuff because her dad wouldn't let her go anywhere with a guy alone (even a totally harmless guy like Aaron Ben-Simon, whose neck was as thick as my upper arm), but when we went with her she sort of ignored us, which I guess is the point. Only for the two weeks they went out, you sort of couldn't talk to Shameeka, because all she could talk about was Aaron.

Not that all my mom can talk about is Mr. Gianini. She's not like that at all. But I had a feeling if I went to Central Park I might have to see kissing. Not that there's anything wrong with kissing, like on TV. When it's your mom and your Algebra teacher, though . . .

You know what I mean, right?

REASONS I SHOULD MAKE UP WITH LILLY

1. We've been best friends since kindergarten.
2. One of us has to be the bigger person and make the first move.
3. She makes me laugh.
4. Who else can I eat lunch with?
5. I miss her.

REASONS I SHOULD NOT MAKE UP WITH LILLY

1. She's always telling me what to do.
2. She thinks she knows everything.
3. Lilly is the one who started it, so she should be the one to apologize.
4. I will never achieve self-actualization if I always back down from my convictions.
5. What if I apologize and she STILL won't talk to me????

Even Later on Sunday

I just turned on my computer to look up some stuff about Afghanistan on the Internet (I have to write a paper for World Civ on a current event), and then I saw that someone was instant messaging me. I hardly ever get instant messages, so I was totally excited.

But then I saw who it was from: CracKing.

Michael Moscovitz? What could *he* want?

Here's what he wrote:

CracKing: Hey, Thermopolis. What happened to you last night? It's like you went mental, or something.

Me? Mental???

FtLouie: For your information, I did not go mental. I just got tired of your sister always telling me what to do. Not that it's any of your business.

CracKing: What are you being so snotty about? Of course it's my business. I have to live with her, don't I?

FtLouie: Why? Is she talking about me?

CracKing: You could say that.

I can't believe she's been talking about me. And you

know she can't have been saying anything good.

FtLouie: What's she saying?

CracKing: I thought it wasn't any of my business.

I'm so glad I don't have a brother.

FtLouie: It isn't. What's she saying about me?

CracKing: That she doesn't know what's with you these days, but ever since your dad came to visit you've been acting like a head case.

FtLouie: Me? A head case? What about her? She's the one who's always criticizing me. I'm so sick of it!! If she wants to be my friend, why can't she just accept me the way I am???

CracKing: No need to yell.

FtLouie: I'm not yelling!!!

CracKing: You're using excessive amounts of punctuation, and on-line, that's like yelling. Besides, she's not the only one criticizing. She says you won't support her boycott of Ho's Deli.

FtLouie: Well, she's right. I won't. It's stupid. Don't you think it's stupid?

CracKing: Sure it's stupid. Are you still flunking Algebra?

That was out of the blue.

FtLouie: I guess so. But considering the fact that Mr. G slept over last night, I'll probably scrape by with a D. Why?

CracKing: What? Mr. G slept over? At your place? What was that like?

Now, why did I tell him that? It'll be all over school by tomorrow morning. Maybe Mr. G will get fired! I don't know if teachers are allowed to date their pupils' mothers. Why did I tell Michael that?

FtLouie: It was pretty awful. But then he kind of joked around, and made it okay. I don't know. I should probably be more mad, but my mom's so happy, it's hard.

CracKing: Your mom could do a lot worse than Mr. G. Imagine if she was going out with Mr. Stuart.

Mr. Stuart teaches Health. He thinks he's God's gift to women. I haven't had him yet, since you don't have Health until sophomore year, but even I know that you should never go near Mr. Stuart's desk, because if you do, he'll reach out and rub your shoulders like he's giving you a massage, but everybody says he's really just trying to see whether or not you're wearing a bra.

If my mom ever went out with Mr. Stuart, I would move to Afghanistan.

FTLOUIE: Ha ha ha. Why'd you want to know whether or not I'm flunking Algebra?

CRACKING: Oh, because I'm done with this month's issue of Crackhead, and I thought if you wanted, I could tutor you during G & T. If you wanted.

Michael Moscovitz, offering to do something for me? I couldn't believe it. I nearly fell off my computer chair.

FTLOUIE: Wow, that would be great! Thanks!

CRACKING: Don't mention it. Hang in there, Thermopolis.

Then he signed off.
Can you believe it? Wasn't that nice? I wonder what's got into him.
I should definitely fight with Lilly more often.

Just when I thought things might be looking very slightly up, my dad called. He said he was sending Lars over to pick me up so me and him and Grandmère could have dinner together at the Plaza.

Notice the invitation didn't include Mom.

But I guess that's okay, since Mom didn't want to go anyway. When I told her I was going she got really cheerful, in fact.

"Oh, that's okay," she said. "I'll just stay here and order in some Thai food and watch *Sixty Minutes*."

She's been really cheerful ever since she got back from Central Park. She says she and Mr. G went on one of those dorky carriage rides. I was shocked. Those carriage drivers don't take care of their horses at all. There's always some ancient carriage horse keeling over from lack of water. I had always vowed never to ride in one of those carriages. At least not until they start giving those horses some rights, and I always thought my mom agreed with me.

Love can do strange things to people.

The Plaza wasn't that bad this time. I guess I'm getting used to it. The doormen know who I am now—or at least they know who Lars is—so they don't give me a hard time anymore. Grandmère and my dad were both in kind of bad moods. I don't know why. I guess they're not getting paid to spend time with each other, like I kind of am.

Dinner was *so* boring. Grandmère went on and on about which fork to use with what and why. There were all these courses, and most of them were meat. One was fish, though, so I ate that, plus dessert, which was a big fancy tower of chocolate. Grandmère tried to tell me that when I am representing Genovia at state functions I have to eat whatever is put down in front of me or I will insult my hosts and possibly create an international incident. But I told her I would have my staff explain to my hosts ahead of time that I don't eat meat, so not to serve me any.

Grandmère looked kind of mad. I guess it never occurred to her that I might have watched that made-for-TV movie about Princess Diana. I know all about how to get out of eating stuff at state dinners, and also about barfing up what you did eat afterwards (only I would never do that).

All through dinner, Dad kept asking me these weird questions about Mom. Like was I uncomfortable about her relationship with Mr. Gianini, and did I want him to say something to her. I think he was trying to get me to tell him whether or not I thought it was serious between the two of them—Mr. G and my mom, I mean.

Well, I know it's pretty serious if he's spending the night. My mom only lets guys she really, really likes spend the night. So far, including Mr. G, that's only been three guys in the past fourteen years: Wolfgang, who turned out to be gay; this guy Tim, who turned out to be a Republican; and now my Algebra teacher. That's not so many, really. It's only like one guy every four years.

Or something like that.

But of course I couldn't tell my dad that Mr. G had spent the night, or I know he'd have had an embolism. He is such a chauvinist—he has girlfriends stay over at Miragnac every summer, sometimes a new one every two weeks!—but he expects Mom to stay pure as the driven snow.

If Lilly were still speaking to me, I know she'd say men are such hypocrites.

A part of me wanted to tell my dad about Mr. G, just so he'd stop being so smug. But I didn't want to give my grandmother any more ammunition against my mom—Grandmère says my mom is "flighty"—so I just pretended like I didn't know anything about it.

Grandmère says we're going to work on my vocabulary tomorrow. She says my French is atrocious but my English is even worse. She says if she ever hears me say "*Whatever*" again, she's going to wash my mouth out with soap.

I said, "Whatever, Grandmère," and she shot me this way dirty look. I wasn't trying to be smart-alecky, though. I really forgot.

To date, I've made $200 for Greenpeace. I'm probably going to go down in history as the girl who saved all the whales.

When I got home, I noticed there were *two* empty containers of pad Thai in the trash. Also *two* sets of plastic chopsticks and *two* bottles of Heineken in the recycling bin. I asked my mom if she'd had Mr. G over for dinner—my God, she'd spent the whole day with him already!—and she said, "Oh, no, honey. I was just really hungry."

That's two lies she's told me in one day. This thing with Mr. G must be pretty serious.

Lilly still hasn't called. I'm starting to think maybe *I* should call *her*. But what would I say? *I* didn't do anything. I mean, I know I told her to shut up, but that was only because she told me I was turning into Lana Weinberger. I had every right to tell her to shut up.

Or did I? Maybe nobody has a right to tell anybody to shut up. Maybe this is how wars get started, because someone tells someone else to shut up, and then no one will apologize.

If this keeps up, who am I going to eat lunch with tomorrow?

When Lars pulled up in front of Lilly's building to pick her up for school, her doorman said she'd already left. Talk about holding a grudge.

This is the longest fight we've ever had.

When I walked into school, the first thing somebody did was shove a petition in my face.

BOYCOTT HO'S DELI!
SIGN BELOW AND TAKE A
STAND AGAINST RACISM!

I said I wouldn't sign it, and Boris, who was the person holding it, told me I was ungrateful, and that in the country he came from voices raised in protest had been crushed for years by the government, and that I should feel lucky I lived in a place where I could sign a petition and not live in fear that the secret police would come after me.

I told Boris that in America we don't tuck our sweaters into our pants.

One thing you have to say for Lilly: She acts fast. The whole school is plastered with Boycott Ho's Deli posters.

The other thing you have to say about Lilly: When she's mad, she stays mad. She is totally not speaking to me.

I wish Mr. G would get off my case. Who *cares* about integers, anyway?

Operations on Real Numbers: negatives or opposites—numbers on opposite sides of the zero but the same distance from zero on the number line are called negatives or opposites

What to Do During Algebra

O what to do during Algebra!
The possibilities are limitless:
There's drawing, and yawning,
and portable chess.

There's dozing, and dreaming,
and feeling confused.
There's humming, and strumming,
and looking bemused.

You can stare at the clock.
You can hum a little song.
I've tried just about everything
to pass the time along.

BUT NOTHING WORKS!!!!!

So even if Lilly and I weren't in a fight, I wouldn't have been able to sit with her at lunch today. She's become the queen of the cause célèbre. All these people were clustered around the table where she and I and Shameeka and Ling Su normally eat our dumplings from Big Wong. *Boris Pelkowski* was sitting where I usually sit.

Lilly must be in heaven. She's always wanted to be worshiped by a musical genius.

So I was standing there like a total idiot with my stupid tray of stupid salad, which was the only vegetarian entree today, since they ran out of cans of Sterno for the bean and grain bar, and I was like, Who am *I* going to sit by? There are only about ten tables in our caf, since we have rotating lunch shifts: There's the table where I sit with Lilly, and then the jock table, the cheerleader table, the rich kid table, the hip-hop table, the druggie table, the drama freak table, the National Honor Society table, the foreign exchange students table, and the table where Tina Hakim Baba sits every day with her bodyguard.

I couldn't sit with the jocks or the cheerleaders, because I'm not either. I couldn't sit at the rich kids' table because I don't have a cell phone or a broker. I'm not into hip-hopping or drugs, I didn't get a part in the latest play, and with my F in Algebra the chance of my getting into the National Honor Society is like nil, and I can't understand anything the foreign exchange students say since there are no French ones.

I looked at Tina Hakim Baba. She had a salad in front of her, just like me. Only Tina eats salad because she has a weight problem, not because she's a vegetarian. She was reading a romance novel. It had a photograph on the front of a teenage boy with his arms around a teenage girl. The teenage girl had long blond hair and pretty big breasts for someone with such thin thighs. She looked exactly the way I know my grandmother wants me to look.

I walked over and put my tray down in front of Tina Hakim Baba's.

"Can I sit here?" I asked.

Tina looked up from her book. She had an expression of total shock on her face. She looked at me, and then she looked at her bodyguard. He was a tall, dark-skinned man in a black suit. He had on sunglasses even though we were inside. I think Lars could probably have taken him, if it had come down to a fight between the two of them.

When Tina looked at her bodyguard, he looked at me—at least I think he did; it was hard to tell with those sunglasses—and nodded.

Tina smiled really big at me. "Please," she said, laying down her book. "Sit with me."

I sat down. I felt kind of bad, seeing Tina smile like

156

that. Like maybe I should have asked to sit down with her before. But I used to think she was such a freak because she rode to school in a limo and had a bodyguard.

I don't think she's as much of a freak now.

Tina and I ate our salads and talked about how much school food sucks. She told me about her diet. Her mother put her on it. She wants to lose twenty pounds by the Cultural Diversity Dance. But the Cultural Diversity Dance is this Saturday, so I don't know how that's going to work out for her. I asked Tina if she had a date for the Cultural Diversity Dance or something, and she got all giggly and said yes she did. She's going with a guy from Trinity, which is another private school in Manhattan. The guy's name is Dave Farouq El-Abar.

Hello? It isn't fair. Even Tina Hakim Baba, whose father doesn't allow her to walk two blocks to school, has been asked out by someone.

Well, she's got breasts, so I guess that's why.

Tina is pretty nice. When she got up to go to the jet line to get another diet soda—the bodyguard went with her; God, if Lars ever started shadowing me like that, I'd kill myself—I read the back of her book. The book was called *I Think My Name Is Amanda*, and it was about a girl who woke up from a coma and couldn't remember who she was. This really cute boy comes to visit her in the hospital and tells her that her name is Amanda and that he's her boyfriend. She spends the rest of the book trying to figure out whether or not he's lying.

I am so sure! If some cute boy wants to tell you that he's your boyfriend, why wouldn't you just *let* him? Some girls don't know when they've got it made.

While I was reading the back of the book, this shadow fell over it, and I looked up and there was Lana Weinberger. It must have been a game day, because she had on her cheerleader uniform, a green-and-white pleated miniskirt and a tight white sweater with a giant *A* across the front of it. I think she stuffs her pom-poms down her bra when she isn't using them. Otherwise, I don't see how her chest could stick out so much.

"Nice hair, Amelia," she said in her snotty voice. "Who are you supposed to be? Tank Girl?"

I looked past her. Josh Richter was standing there with some of his dumb jock friends. They weren't paying any attention to me and Lana. They were talking about a party they'd been to over the weekend. They were all "wrecked" from having consumed too much beer.

I wonder if their coach knows.

"What do you call this color, anyway?" Lana wanted to know. She touched the top of my head. "Pus yellow?"

Tina Hakim Baba and her bodyguard came back while Lana was standing there tormenting me. In addition to her diet soda, Tina had purchased a Nutty Royale ice cream cone, which she gave to me. I thought this was very nice of her, considering the fact that I'd hardly ever spoken to her before.

But Lana didn't see the niceness of this gesture. Instead she asked, all innocently, "Oh, Tina, did you buy that ice cream for Amelia here? Did your daddy give you an extra hundred dollars today so you could buy yourself a new friend?"

Tina's dark eyes filled up with hurt. The bodyguard saw this and opened his mouth.

Then a strange thing happened. I was sitting there, looking at the tears welling up in Tina Hakim Baba's eyes, and then the next thing I knew, I'd taken my Nutty Royale and thrust it with all my might at the front of Lana's sweater.

Lana looked down at the vanilla ice cream, hard chocolate shell, and peanuts that were sticking to her chest. Josh Richter and the other jocks stopped talking and looked at Lana's chest, too. The noise level in the cafeteria plummeted to the quietest I've heard it. *Everyone* was looking at the ice cream cone sticking to Lana's chest. It was so quiet I could hear Boris breathing through the wires of his bionater.

Then Lana started to scream.

"You—you—" I guess she couldn't think of a word bad enough to call me. "You—you . . . Look what you've done! Look what you've done to my sweater!"

I stood up and grabbed my tray. "Come on, Tina," I said. "Let's go somewhere a little bit quieter."

Tina, her big brown eyes on the sugar cone sticking out of the middle of the *A* on Lana's chest, picked up her tray and followed me. The bodyguard followed Tina. I could swear he was laughing.

As Tina and I walked past the table where Lilly and I usually sat, I saw Lilly staring at me with her mouth open. She had obviously seen the whole thing.

Well, I guess she's going to have to change her diagnosis: I am *not* unassertive. Not when I don't want to be.

I'm not sure, but as Tina and her bodyguard and I left, I thought I heard some applause coming from the geek table.

I think self-actualization might be right around the corner.

Oh my God. I am in so much trouble. Nothing like this has ever happened to me before!

I am sitting in the principal's office!

That's right. I got sent to the principal's office for stabbing Lana Weinberger with a Nutty Royale!

I should have known she'd tell on me. She is such a big whiner.

I'm kind of scared. I've never disobeyed a student rule before. I've always been a really good kid. When the student worker came to our G and T class with the pink hall pass, I never thought for a minute it might be for me. I was sitting there with Michael Moscovitz. He was showing me that the way I subtract is all wrong. He says my main problem is that I don't write my numbers neat enough when borrowing. Also that I don't keep track of my notes, and scribble them in whatever notebook I happen to have handy. He says I should keep all my Algebra notes in one notebook.

Also, he says I seem to have trouble concentrating.

But the reason I couldn't concentrate was that I had never sat so close to a boy before! I mean, I realize it was only Michael Moscovitz, and that I see him all the time, and he'd never like me anyway because I'm a freshman and he's a senior, and I'm his little sister's best friend and all—at least, I used to be.

But he's still a boy, a *cute* boy, even if he *is* Lilly's

brother. It was really hard to pay attention to subtraction when I could smell this really nice clean boy smell coming from him. Plus every once in a while he would put his hand over mine and take my pencil away and go, "No, like *this*, Mia."

Of course, I was also having trouble concentrating because I kept feeling like Lilly was looking at us. She wasn't, of course. Now that she's fighting the evil forces of racism in our neighborhood, she doesn't have time for the little people like me. She was sitting at this big table with all of her supporters, plotting their next move in the Ho Offensive. She even let Boris come out of the supply closet to help.

May I point out that he was all over her? How she can stand having his spindly little violin-stroking arm around the back of her chair, I can't imagine. And he *still* hasn't untucked his sweater.

So I really shouldn't have worried that anybody was going to notice me and Michael. I mean, he certainly didn't have his arm around the back of *my* chair. Although once, under the table, his knee touched my knee. I nearly died at the niceness of it all.

Then that stupid hall pass arrived with *my* name on it.

I wonder if I'm going to get expelled. Maybe if I get expelled I could go to a different school, where nobody knows that my hair used to be a different color and that these fingernails aren't really real. That might be kind of nice.

FROM NOW ON I WILL

1. Think before I act.
2. Try to be gracious, no matter how much I am provoked to behave otherwise.
3. Tell the truth, except when doing so would hurt someone's feelings.
4. Stay as far away as possible from Lana Weinberger.

Uh-oh. Principal Gupta is ready to see me now.

Monday Night

Well, I don't know what I'm going to do now. I have detention for a week, *plus* math review with Mr. G, *plus* princess lessons with Grandmère.

I didn't get home until nine o'clock tonight. Something has *got* to give.

My father is furious. He says he is going to sue the school. He says no one can give his daughter detention for defending the weak. I told him that Principal Gupta can. She can do anything. She's the principal.

I can't say I really blame her. I mean, it wasn't like I said I was sorry or anything. Principal Gupta is a nice lady, but what could she do? I admitted I had done it. She told me I'd have to apologize to Lana and pay to have her sweater cleaned. I said I'd pay for the sweater but that I wouldn't apologize. Principal Gupta looked at me over the rims of her bifocals and went, "I beg your pardon, Mia?"

I repeated that I wouldn't apologize. My heart was beating like crazy. I didn't want to make anybody mad, especially Principal Gupta, who can be very scary when she wants to. I tried to picture her in her husband's sweatpants, but it didn't work. She still scared me.

But I won't apologize to Lana. I won't.

Principal Gupta didn't look mad, though. She looked concerned. I guess that's how educators are supposed to look. You know. Concerned about you. She went, "Mia, I must say, when Lana came in here with her complaint, I was extremely surprised. It's usually Lilly Moscovitz I have to pull in here. I never expected I was going to have to pull *you* in. Not for disciplinary reasons. Academic reasons, maybe. I understand you aren't doing very well in Algebra. But I've never known you to be a discipline problem before. I really feel I must ask you, Mia . . . is everything all right?"

For a minute I just stared at her.

Is everything all right? *Is everything all right?*

Hmm, hold on a minute, let me see . . . my mom is going out with my Algebra teacher, a subject I'm flunking, by the way; my best friend hates me; I'm fourteen years old and I've never been asked out; I don't have any breasts; and oh, I just found out I'm the princess of Genovia.

"Oh, sure," I said to Principal Gupta. "Everything is fine."

"Are you certain, Mia? Because I can't help wondering if this isn't all rooted in some problems you might be having . . . maybe at home?"

Who did she think I was, anyway? Lana *Whine*berger? Like I was really going to sit there and tell her my problems. Yeah, Principal Gupta. On top of all that other stuff, my grandmother is in town, and my dad is paying $100 a day for me to get lessons from her in how to be a princess. Oh, and this weekend, I ran into Mr. Gianini in my kitchen, and all he was wearing was a pair of boxer shorts. Anything else you want to know?

"Mia," Principal Gupta said, "I want you to know that you are a very special person. You have many wonderful qualities. There is no reason for you to feel threatened by Lana Weinberger. None at all."

Oh, okay. Just because she's the prettiest, most popular girl in my class, and she's going out with the handsomest, most popular boy in school, you're right, Principal Gupta. There's no reason at all to feel threatened by her. Especially since she puts me down every chance she gets and tries to humiliate me in public. Threatened? *Me?* Nah.

"You know, Mia," Principal Gupta said, "I bet if you took the time to get to know Lana you'd find that she's really a very nice girl. A girl just like you."

Right. Just like me.

I was so upset, I actually told Grandmère all about it at our vocabulary lesson. She was surprisingly sympathetic.

"When I was a girl your age," Grandmère said, "there was a girl just like this Lana at my school. Her name was Genevieve. She sat behind me in Geography. Genevieve would take the end of my braid and dip it in her inkwell, so that when I stood up I got ink all over my dress. But the teacher would never believe me that Genevieve did it on purpose."

"Really?" I was kind of impressed. That Genevieve had some guts. I never met anyone who'd try to dis my grandmother. "What did you do?"

Grandmère let out this evil laugh. "Oh, nothing."

There is no way she did *nothing* to Genevieve. Not with a laugh like that. But no matter how hard I pestered her, Grandmère wouldn't tell me what she did to get back at Genevieve. I'm kind of thinking maybe she killed her.

Well? It could happen.

But I guess I shouldn't have pestered Grandmère so hard, because to shut me up she gave me a quiz! I'm not kidding!

It was really hard, too. I've stapled it in here, since I got a 98. Grandmère says I've really come a long way since we started.

Grandmère's Test

In a restaurant, what does one do with one's napkin when one rises to go to the powder room?
If it's a four-star restaurant, hand it to the waiter who rushes over to help you with your chair. If it's a normal place, and no waiter rushes over, leave your napkin on your empty chair.

Under what circumstances is it acceptable to apply lipstick in public?
Never.

What are the characteristics of capitalism?
Private ownership of the means of production
and distribution, and the exchange of goods
based on the operations of the market.

*What is the appropriate reply to make to a man who
says he loves you?*
Thank you. You are very kind.

*What did Marx consider to be the contradiction in
capitalism?*
The value of any commodity is determined by
the amount of labor needed to produce it. In
denying workers the value of what they have
produced, the capitalists are undermining their
own economic system.

White shoes are unacceptable . . .
At funerals, after Labor Day, before Memorial
Day, and anywhere there might be horses.

Describe an oligarchy.
Small group exercises control for generally
corrupt purposes.

Describe a Sidecar.
⅓ lemon juice, ⅓ Cointreau, ⅓ brandy shaken
well with ice, strained before serving.

The only one I missed was the one about what to say to a man when he tells you he loves you. It turns out you aren't supposed to say thank you.

Not, of course, that this will ever happen to me. But Grandmère says I might be surprised someday.

I wish!

No Lilly again this morning. Not that I expected there to be. But I made Lars stop at her place anyway, just in case maybe she wanted to be friends again. I mean, she could have seen how assertive I was with Lana and decided she was wrong to criticize me so much.

But I guess not.

The funny thing is, when Lars was dropping me off at school, Tina Hakim Baba's chauffeur was dropping her off, too. We sort of smiled at each other, then walked into school together, her bodyguard behind us. Tina said she wanted to thank me for what I had done yesterday. She said she told her parents about it, and that they want me to come over for dinner Friday night.

"And maybe," Tina asked, all shyly, "you could spend the night after, if you wanted."

I said, "Okay." I mostly said it because I feel sorry for Tina, since she doesn't have any other friends, because everybody thinks she's so weird, with the body-guard and all. I also said it because I heard she has a fountain in her house, just like Donald Trump, and I wanted to see if that was true.

And I kind of like her, too. She's *nice* to me.

It's nice to have somebody be nice to you.

I HAVE <u>GOT</u> TO

1. Stop waiting for the phone to ring (Lilly is NOT going to call; neither is Josh Richter)
2. Make more friends
3. Have more self-confidence
4. Stop biting my fake fingernails
5. Start acting more:
    A. Responsible
    B. Adult
    C. Mature
6. Be happier
7. Achieve self-actualization
8. Buy:
    trash bags
    napkins
    conditioner
    tuna
    toilet paper!!!!

Oh my God. I can't even believe this. But it must be true, since Shameeka just told me.

Lilly has a date to the Cultural Diversity Dance this weekend.

Lilly has a date. Even *Lilly* has a date. I thought all the boys in our school were terrified of Lilly.

But there's one boy who's not:

Boris Pelkowski.

AAAAHHHHHHHHHHHHHHHHH!

No boy will ever ask me out. Ever. EVERYONE has a date to the Cultural Diversity Dance: Shameeka, Lilly, Ling Su, Tina Hakim Baba. I'm the only one not going. The ONLY ONE.

Why was I born under such an unlucky star? Why did *I* have to be cursed with such freakishness? Why? WHY???

I would give anything if, instead of being a five-foot-nine flat-chested princess, I could be a five-foot-six normal person with breasts.

ANYTHING.

Satire—employs humor systematically for the purpose of persuasion

Irony—counter to expectation

Parody—close imitation that exaggerates ridiculous or objectionable features

Today in G and T, in between showing me how to carry over, Michael Moscovitz complimented me on my handling of what he called the Weinberger Incident. I was surprised he'd heard about it. He said it was all over school, about how I'd decimated Lana in front of Josh. He said, "Your locker is right next to Josh's, isn't it?"

I said yes it was.

He said, "That must be awkward," but I told him actually it wasn't, since Lana seems to be avoiding that area lately, and Josh never talks to me at all, except to say, "Can I get by here?" once in a while.

I asked him if Lilly was still saying mean things about me, and he said, all taken aback, "She's never said mean things about you. She just doesn't understand why you blew up at her like that."

I said, "Michael, she's always putting me down! I just couldn't take it anymore. I have too many other problems without having friends who aren't supportive of me."

He laughed. "What kind of problems could *you* have?"

Like I was too much of a kid or something to have problems!

Boy, did I straighten him out. I couldn't exactly tell him about being the princess of Genovia, or about not having any breasts or anything, but I did remind him that I'm flunking Algebra, I have detention for a week, and I had recently woken up to find Mr. Gianini in his boxer shorts eating breakfast with my mom.

He said he guessed I did have some problems after all.

The whole time Michael and I were talking, I saw Lilly shooting us these looks from behind the poster board she was writing Ho-Gate slogans on with a big black Magic Marker. So I guess because I'm fighting with her I'm not allowed to be friends with her brother.

Or maybe she's just sore because her boycott of Ho's Deli is creating serious turmoil within the school. First of all, all the Asian kids have started doing their shopping exclusively at Ho's. And why not? Because of Lilly's campaign, now they know they can get a five-cent discount on just about anything. The other problem is that there is no other deli within walking distance. This has caused some serious division within the ranks of the protesters. The nonsmokers want to continue the boycott, but the smokers are all for writing the Hos a stern letter and then forgetting about it. And since all the popular kids in school smoke, they aren't honoring the boycott at all. They're going to Ho's just like they always did to get their Camel Lights.

When you can't get the popular kids on your side, you have to realize it's hopeless: Without celebrity supporters, no cause stands a chance. I mean, where would all those starving kids be without Sally Struthers?

Anyway, then Michael asked me a strange question. He went, "So, are you grounded?"

I looked at him kind of funny. "You mean for getting detention? No, of course not. My mom is totally on my side. My dad wants to sue the school."

Michael said, "Oh. Well, I was wondering because, if you aren't busy Saturday, I thought maybe we could—"

But then Mrs. Hill came in and made us all fill out questionnaires for the Ph.D. she's doing on urban youth violence, even though Lilly complained that we're hardly qualified to comment, seeing as how the only youth violence any of us had ever experienced was when there was a sale on relaxed fit jeans at the Gap on Madison Avenue.

Then the bell rang, and I ran out as fast as I could. I knew what Michael was going to ask me, see. He was going to suggest we meet to go over my long division, which he says is a human tragedy. And I just didn't think I could take it. Math? On the weekend? After spending almost every waking moment on it all week?

No, thank you.

But I didn't want to be rude, so I left before he could ask me. Was that terrible of me?

Really, a girl can only take so much criticism on her remainders.

ma	mon	tes
ta	ton	tes
sa	son	ses
notre	notre	nos
votre	votre	vos
leur	leur	leurs

HOMEWORK

Algebra: pg. 121, 1–57 odd only
English: ??? Ask Shameeka
World Civ: questions at end of Chapter 9
G&T: none
French: pour demain, *une vignette culturelle*
Biology: none

Grandmère says Tina Hakim Baba sounds like a much better friend for me than Lilly Moscovitz. But I think she is only saying that because Lilly's parents are psychoanalysts, and it turns out Tina's dad is this Arabian sheikh and her mom is related to the king of Sweden, so they are more appropriate for the heir to the throne of Genovia to hang out with.

The Hakim Babas are also superrich, according to my grandmother. They own about a gazillion oil wells. Grandmère told me when I go have dinner with them on Friday night, I have to bring a gift and wear my Gucci loafers. I asked Grandmère what kind of gift, and she said breakfast. She's special-ordering it from Balducci's and having it delivered Saturday morning.

Being a princess is hard work.

I just remembered: At lunch today Tina had a new book with her. It had a cover just like the last one, only this time the heroine was a brunette. This one was called *My Secret Love*, and it was about a girl from the wrong side of the tracks who falls in love with a rich boy who never notices her. Then the girl's uncle kidnaps the boy and holds him for ransom, and she has to bathe his wounds and help him to escape and stuff, and of course he falls madly in love with her. Tina said she already read the end, and the girl gets to go and live with the rich boy's parents after her uncle goes to jail and can no longer support her.

How come things like that don't ever happen to *me*?

No Lilly again today. Lars suggested we'd make better time if we just drove straight to school and didn't stop by her place every day. I guess he's right.

It was really weird when we pulled up to Albert Einstein. All the people who normally hang around outside before school starts, smoking and sitting on Joe, the stone lion, were all clustered into these groups looking at something. I suppose somebody's dad has been accused of money laundering again. Parents can be so self-centered: Before they do something illegal, they should totally stop and think about how their kids are going to feel if they get caught.

If I were Chelsea Clinton, I would change my name and move to Iceland.

I just walked right on by to show I wasn't going to have any part in gossip. A bunch of people stared at me. I guess Michael's right: It really *has* gotten around, about me stabbing Lana with that Nutty Royale. Either that or my hair was sticking up in some weird way. But I checked in the mirror in the girls' room and it wasn't.

A bunch of girls ran out of the bathroom giggling like crazy when I went in, though.

Sometimes I wish I lived on a desert island. Really. With nobody else around for hundreds of miles. Just me, the ocean, the sand, and a coconut tree.

And maybe a high-definition 37-inch TV with a

satellite dish and a Sony PlayStation with Bandicoot,
for when I get bored.

LITTLE KNOWN FACTS

1. The most commonly asked question at Albert
   Einstein High School is "Do you have any
   gum?"
2. Bees and bulls are attracted to the color red.
3. In my homeroom, it sometimes takes up to half
   an hour just to take attendance.
4. I miss being best friends with Lilly Moscovitz.

This totally weird thing happened. Josh Richter came up to his locker to put his Trig book away, and he said, "How you doin'?" to me as I was getting out my Algebra notebook.

I swear to God I am not making this up.

I was in such total shock, I nearly dropped my backpack. I don't have any idea what I said to him. I think I said I was fine. I *hope* I said I was fine.

Why is Josh Richter speaking to me?

It must have been another one of those synaptic breakdowns, like the one he had at Bigelows.

Then Josh slammed his locker closed, *looked right down into my face*—he's really tall—and said, "See you later."

Then he walked away.

It took me five minutes to stop hyperventilating.

His eyes are so blue they hurt to look at.

It's over.

I'm dead.

That's it.

Now I know what everyone was looking at outside. I know why they were whispering and giggling. I know why those girls ran out of the bathroom. I know why Josh Richter talked to me.

My picture is on the cover of the *Post*.

That's right. The *New York Post*. Read by millions of New Yorkers daily.

Oh, yeah. I'm dead.

It's a pretty good picture of me, actually. I guess somebody took it as I was leaving the Plaza Sunday night, after dinner with Grandmère and my dad. I'm going down the steps just outside the revolving door. I'm sort of smiling, only not at the camera. I don't remember anybody taking my picture, but I guess somebody did.

Superimposed over the photo are the words *Princess Amelia*, and then in smaller letters *New York's Very Own Royal*.

Great. Just great.

Mr. Gianini was the one who figured it out. He said he was walking to catch the subway to work and he saw it on the newsstand. He called my mother. My mom was taking a shower, though, and didn't hear the phone. Mr.

G left a message. But my mom never checks the machine in the morning, because everyone who knows her knows she is not a morning person, so nobody ever calls before noon. When Mr. G called again, she had already left for her studio, where she never answers the phone, because she wears a Walkman when she paints, so she can listen to Howard Stern.

So then Mr. G had no choice but to call my dad at the Plaza, which was pretty nervy of him, if you think about it. According to Mr. G, my dad blew a gasket. He told Mr. G that until he could get there, I should be sent to the principal's office, where I would be "safe."

My dad has obviously never met Principal Gupta.

Actually, I shouldn't say that. She hasn't been so bad. She showed me the paper and said, kind of sarcastically, but in a nice way, "You might have shared this with me, Mia, when I asked you the other day if everything was all right at home."

I blushed. "Well," I said, "I didn't think anybody would believe me."

"It is," Principal Gupta said, "a bit unbelievable."

That's what the story on page 2 of the *Post* said, too. FAIRY TALE COMES TRUE FOR ONE LUCKY NEW YORK KID was how the reporter, one Ms. Carol Fernandez, put it. Like I had won the lottery, or something. Like I should be *happy* about it.

Ms. Carol Fernandez went on at length about my mom, "the raven-haired avant-garde painter Helen

Thermopolis," and about my dad, "the handsome Prince Phillipe of Genovia," who'd "successfully battled his way back from a bout of testicular cancer." Oh, thanks, Carol Fernandez, for letting all of New York know my dad's only got one you-know-what.

Then she went on to describe me as "the statuesque beauty who is the product of Helen and Phillipe's tempestuous whirlwind college romance."

HELLO??? CAROL FERNANDEZ, ARE YOU ON CRACK????

I am NOT a statuesque beauty. Yeah, I'm TALL. I'm way TALL. But I am no beauty. I want what Carol Fernandez has been smoking, if she thinks *I'M* beautiful.

No wonder everybody was laughing at me. This is SO embarrassing. I mean, really.

Oh, here comes my dad. Boy, does *he* look mad. . . .

It isn't fair.

This is totally, completely unfair.

I mean, anybody else's dad would have let them come home. Anybody else's dad, if his kid's picture was on the front of the *Post*, would say, "Maybe you should skip school for a few days until things calm down."

Anybody else's dad would have been like, "Maybe you should change schools. How do you feel about Iowa? Would you like to go to school in Iowa?"

But oh, no. Not *my* dad. Because *he's* a prince. And he says members of the royal family of Genovia do not "go home" when there is a crisis. No, they stay where they are and slug it out.

Slug it out. I think my dad has something in common with Carol Fernandez: They're BOTH on crack.

Then my dad reminded me that it's not like I'm not getting paid for this. Right! One hundred lousy bucks! One hundred lousy bucks a day to be publicly ridiculed and humiliated.

Those baby seals better be grateful, that's all I have to say.

So here I am in English, and everybody is whispering about me and pointing at me like I'm a victim of alien abduction or something, and my dad expects me to sit here and let them, because I'm a princess and that's what princesses do.

But these kids are *brutal*.

I tried to tell my dad that. I was like, "Dad, you don't understand. They're all laughing at me."

And all he said was, "I'm sorry, honey. You're just going to have to tough it out. You knew this was going to happen eventually. I'd hoped it wouldn't be quite this soon, but it's probably just as well to get it over with. . . ."

Um, hello? I did *not* know this was going to happen eventually. I thought I was going to be able to keep this whole princess thing a secret. My lovely plan about only being a princess in Genovia is falling apart. I have to be a princess right here in Manhattan, and believe me, that is no picnic.

I was so mad at my dad for telling me I had to go back to class, I accused him of having ratted me out to Carol Fernandez himself.

He got all offended. "*Me?* I don't know any Carol Fernandez." He shot this funny look at Mr. Gianini, who was standing there with his hands in his pockets, looking all concerned.

"What?" Mr. G said, going from concerned to surprised real fast. "*Me?* I'd never even *heard* of Genovia until this morning."

"Geez, Dad," I said. "Don't blame Mr. G. *He* had nothing to do with it."

My dad didn't look very convinced. "Well, *somebody* leaked the story to the press. . . ." He said it in this mean way, too. You could totally tell he thought Mr. G had done it. But it couldn't have been Mr. Gianini. Carol Fernandez wrote about stuff in her story that there's no way Mr. G could know, because even *Mom* doesn't know about it. Like how Miragnac has a private airstrip. I never told her about that.

But when I told my dad that, he just shot Mr. G a suspicious look. "Well," he said again. "I'm just going to give this Carol Fernandez a call and see who her source is."

And while my dad was doing that, I got stuck with Lars. I'm not kidding. Just like Tina Hakim Baba, I now have a bodyguard trailing around after me from class to class. Like I'm not enough of a laughingstock already.

I now have an armed escort.

I totally tried to get out of it. I was like, "Dad, I can seriously take care of myself," but he was completely rigid and said that even though Genovia is a small country, it is a very wealthy country, and he cannot take the risk of my being kidnapped and held for ransom like the boy in *My Secret Love*, only my dad didn't say that because he's never read *My Secret Love*.

I said, "Dad, no one is going to kidnap me. This is *school*," but he wouldn't go for it. He asked Principal Gupta if it was all right, and she said, "Of course, Your Highness."

Your Highness! Principal Gupta called my dad Your

Highness! If it hadn't been all serious and stuff, I would have wet my pants laughing.

The only good thing that has come out of this is that Principal Gupta let me off detention for the rest of the week, claiming that having my picture in the *Post* is punishment enough.

But really the only reason is that she is totally charmed by my father. He pulled such a Jean-Luc Picard on her, you wouldn't believe it, calling her Madam Principal and apologizing for all the fuss. I practically expected him to kiss her hand, he was flirting so hard with her. And Principal Gupta has been married a million years, and has this big black mole on the side of her nose. And she totally fell for it! She was eating it up!

I wonder if Tina Hakim Baba will still sit with me at lunch. Well, if she does, at least our bodyguards will have something to do: They can compare civilian defense tactics.

I guess I should have my picture on the front of the *Post* more often.

Suddenly I am very popular.

I walked into the cafeteria (I told Lars to keep five paces behind me at all times; he kept stepping on the backs of my combat boots), and Lana Weinberger, of all people, came up to me while I was in the jet line getting my tray, and said, "Hey, Mia. Why don't you come and sit with us?"

I am not even kidding. That lousy hypocrite wants to be friends with me now that I'm a princess.

Tina was right behind me in line (well, Lars was behind me; Tina was behind Lars, and Tina's bodyguard was behind her). But did Lana invite Tina to join her? Of course not. The *New York Post* hadn't called *Tina* a "statuesque beauty." Short, heavyset girls—even one whose father is an Arab sheikh—aren't good enough to sit by *Lana*. Oh, no. Only purebred Genovian princesses are good enough to sit by *Lana*.

I nearly threw up all over my lunch tray.

"No, thanks, Lana," I said. "I already have someone to sit with."

You should have seen Lana's face. The last time I saw her look that shocked, a sugar cone had been stuck to her chest.

Later, when we were sitting down, Tina could only

nibble at her salad. She hadn't said a word about the princess thing. Meanwhile, though, everybody in the whole cafeteria—including the geeks, who never notice anything—were staring at our table. Let me tell you, it was way uncomfortable. I could feel Lilly's eyes boring into me. She hadn't said anything to me yet, but I think she had to have known. Nothing much escapes Lilly.

Anyway, after a while I couldn't stand it anymore. I put down a forkful of rice and beans and said, "Look, Tina. If you don't want to sit with me anymore, I understand."

Tina's big eyes filled up with tears. I mean it. She shook her head, and her long black braid swayed. "What do you mean?" she asked. "You don't like me anymore, Mia?"

It was my turn to be shocked. "What? Of course I like you. I thought maybe you might not like *me*. I mean, everyone is staring at us. I could see why you might not want to sit with me."

Tina smiled sadly. "Everyone always stares at me," she said. "Because of Wahim, you see."

Wahim is her bodyguard. Wahim and Lars were sitting next to us, arguing over whose gun had the most firepower, Wahim's 357 Magnum or Lars's 9mm Glock. It was kind of a disturbing topic, but they both seemed happy as could be. In a minute or two, I expected they'd start to arm wrestle.

"So you see," Tina said, "*I'm* used to people thinking I'm weird. It's *you* I feel sorry for, Mia. You could be sitting with anyone—anyone in this whole cafeteria—and yet you're stuck with me. I don't want you to feel you have to be nice to me just because no one else is."

I got really mad then. Not at Tina. But at everybody else at Albert Einstein. I mean, Tina Hakim Baba is really, really nice, and no one knows it because no one ever talks to her, because she isn't very thin and she's kind of quiet and she's stuck with a stupid bodyguard. While people are worrying about things like the fact that a deli is overcharging some people by five cents for gingko biloba rings, there are human beings walking around our school in abject misery because no one will even say Good morning to them, or How was your weekend?

And then I felt guilty, because a week ago *I* had been one of those people. I had always thought Tina Hakim Baba was a freak. The whole reason I hadn't wanted anyone to find out I was a princess was that I was afraid they'd treat *me* the way they treated Tina Hakim Baba. And now that I know Tina, I know just how wrong I'd been to think badly of her.

So I told Tina I didn't want to sit with anybody but her. I told her I thought we needed to stick together, and not just for the obvious reason (Wahim and Lars). I told her we needed to stick together because everyone else at this stupid school is completely NUTS.

Tina looked a lot happier then, and started filling

me in on the new book she's reading. This one is called *Love Only Once*, and it's about a girl who falls in love with a boy who has terminal cancer. I told Tina it seemed like kind of a bummer thing to read, but she told me she'd already read the end, and that the boy's terminal cancer goes away. So I guess that's okay then.

As we cleared our trays, I saw Lilly staring in my direction. It wasn't the kind of stare someone who was about to apologize would use. So I wasn't too surprised when later, after I got to G and T, Lilly sat there and stared at me some more. Boris kept on trying to talk to her, but she obviously wasn't listening. Finally he gave up and picked up his violin and went back into the supply closet, where he belongs.

Meanwhile, this is how my tutoring session with Lilly's brother went:

Me: Hi, Michael. I did all those problems you gave me. But I still don't see why you couldn't just look at the train schedule to find out what time a train traveling at 67 miles per hour will arrive in Fargo, North Dakota, if it leaves Salt Lake City at 7 A.M.

Michael: So. Princess of Genovia, huh? Were you ever going to share that little piece of info with the group, or were we all supposed to guess?

Me: I was kind of hoping no one would ever find out.

Michael: Well, that's obvious. I don't see why, though. It's not like it's a bad thing.

Me: Are you kidding me? Of course it's bad!

Michael: Did you *read* the article in today's *Post*, Thermopolis?

Me: No way. I'm not going to read that trash. I don't know who this Carol Fernandez thinks she is, but—

Then Lilly got into the act. It was like she couldn't stand not to get involved.

Lilly: So you're not aware that the crown prince of Genovia—namely, your father—has a total personal worth which, including real estate property and the palace's art collection, is estimated at over three hundred million dollars?

Well, I guess it's pretty obvious that *Lilly* read the article in today's *Post*.

Me: Um . . .

Hello? Three hundred million dollars?? And I get a lousy $100 a day???

Lilly: I wonder how much of that fortune was amassed by taking advantage of the sweat of the common laborer.

Michael: Considering that the people of Genovia have traditionally never paid income or property taxes, I would say none of it. What is *with* you, anyway, Lil?

Lilly: Well, if *you* want to tolerate the excesses of the monarchy, you can be my guest, Michael. But I happen to think that it's disgusting, with the world economy in the state it's in today, for anyone to have a total worth of three hundred million dollars . . . especially someone who never did a day's work for it!

Michael: Pardon me, Lilly, but it's my understanding that Mia's father works extremely hard for his country. His father's historic pledge, after Mussolini's forces invaded in 1939, to exercise the rights of sovereignty in accordance with the political and economic interests of neighboring France in exchange for military and naval protection in the event of war might have tied the hands of a lesser politician, but Mia's father has managed to work around that agreement. His efforts have resulted in a nation that has the highest literacy rate in Europe, some of the best educational attainment rates, and the lowest infant mortality, inflation, and unemployment rates in the Western Hemisphere.

I could only stare at Michael after that. *Wow.* Why doesn't Grandmère teach me stuff like *that* at our princess lessons? I mean, this is information I could actually use. I don't exactly need to know which direction to tip my soup bowl. I need to know how to defend myself from virulent antiroyalists like my ex–best friend Lilly.

Lilly: (to Michael) Shut up. (to me) I see they already have you spouting off their populist propaganda like a good little girl.

Me: Me? Michael's the one who—

Michael: Aw, Lilly, you're just jealous.

Lilly: I am not!

Michael: Yes, you are. You're jealous because she

got her hair cut without consulting you. You're jealous because you stopped talking to her and she went out and got a new friend. And you're jealous because all this time Mia's had this secret she didn't tell you.

Lilly: Michael, SHUT UP!

Boris: (leaning out of the supply closet door) Lilly? Did you say something?

Lilly: I WASN'T TALKING TO YOU, BORIS!

Boris: Sorry. (goes back into closet)

Lilly: (really mad now) Gosh, Michael, you sure are quick to come to Mia's defense all of a sudden. I wonder if maybe it ever occurred to you that your argument, while ostensibly based on logic, might have less intellectual than libidinous roots.

Michael: (turning red for some reason) Well, what about your persecution of the Hos? Is that rooted in intellectual reasoning? Or is it more an example of vanity run amok?

Lilly: That's a circular argument.

Michael: It isn't. It's empirical.

Wow. Michael and Lilly are so smart. Grandmère's right: I need to improve my vocabulary.

Michael: (to me) So does this guy (he pointed at Lars) have to follow you around everywhere from now on?

Me: Yes.

Michael: Really? *Everywhere?*

Me: Everywhere except the ladies' room. Then he waits outside.

Michael: What if you were to go on a date? Like to the Cultural Diversity Dance this weekend?

Me: That hasn't exactly been an issue, considering that no one's asked me.

Boris: (leaning out of the supply closet) Excuse me. I accidentally knocked over a bottle of rubber cement with my bow, and it's getting hard to breathe. Can I come out now?

Everyone in the G and T room: NO!!!

Mrs. Hill: (poking her head in from the hallway) What's all this noise in here? We can hardly hear ourselves think in the teachers' lounge. Boris, why are you in the supply closet? Come out now. Everybody else, get back to work!

I need to take a closer look at that article in today's *Post.* Three hundred million dollars?? That's as much as Oprah made last year!

So if we're so rich, how come the TV in my room is only black and white?

Note to self: Look up the words *empirical* and *libidinous*

Wednesday Night

No wonder my dad was so mad about Carol Fernandez's article! When Lars and I walked out of Albert Einstein after my review session there were reporters all over the place. I am not even kidding. It was just like I was a murderer, or a celebrity, or something.

According to Mr. Gianini, who walked out with us, reporters have been arriving all day. There were vans there from New York One, Fox News, CNN, *Entertainment Tonight*—you name it. They've been trying to interview all the kids who go to Albert Einstein, asking them if they know me (for once, being unpopular pays off; I can't imagine they were able to find anybody who could actually remember who I was—at least, not with my new nontriangular hair). Mr. G says Principal Gupta finally had to call the police, because Albert Einstein High is private property and the reporters were trespassing all over, dropping cigarette butts on the steps and blocking the sidewalk and leaning on Joe and stuff.

Which, if you think about it, is exactly what all the popular kids do when they hang around the school grounds after the last bell rings, and Principal Gupta never calls the cops on *them* . . . but then again, I guess their parents are paying tuition.

I have to say, I sort of know now how Princess Diana

must have felt. I mean, when Lars and Mr. G and I came out, the reporters started trying to swarm all over, waving microphones at us and yelling stuff like, "Amelia, how about a smile?" and "Amelia, what's it like to wake up one morning the product of a single-parent family and go to bed the next night a royal princess worth over three hundred million dollars?"

I was kind of scared. Even if I'd wanted to, I couldn't have answered their questions, because I didn't know which microphone to talk into. Plus I was practically rendered blind by all the flashbulbs going off in front of my face.

Then Lars went into action. You should have seen it. First, he told me not to say anything. Then he put his arm around me. He told Mr. G to put his arm around my other side. Then, I don't know how, but we ducked our heads and barreled through all the cameras and microphones and the people attached to them, until the next thing I knew, Lars was pushing me into the backseat of my dad's car and jumping in after me.

Hello! I guess all that training in the Israeli army paid off. (I overheard Lars telling Wahim that's where he'd learned how to work an Uzi. Wahim and Lars actually have some mutual friends, it turns out. I guess all bodyguards go to the same training school out in the Gobi Desert.)

Anyway, as soon as Lars slammed the back door shut, he said "Drive," and the guy behind the wheel hit the gas. I didn't recognize him, but sitting in the passenger seat beside him was my dad. And while we're pulling away, brakes squealing, flashbulbs going off, reporters jumping onto the windshield to get a better shot, my dad goes, all casual, "So. How was your day, Mia?"

Geez!

I decided to ignore my dad. Instead, I turned around in my seat to wave good-bye to Mr. G. Only Mr. G had been swallowed up in a sea of microphones! He wouldn't talk to them, though. He just kept waving his hands at them and trying to head for the subway, so he could take the E train home.

I felt sorry for poor Mr. Gianini then. True, he had probably stuck his tongue in my mom's mouth, but he's a really nice guy and doesn't deserve to be harassed by the media.

I said so to my dad, also that we should have given Mr. G a ride home, and he just got huffy and tugged on his seat belt. He said, "Damn these things. They always choke me."

So then I asked my dad where I was going to go to school now.

My dad looked at me like I was nuts. "You said you wanted to stay at Albert Einstein!" he kind of yelled.

I said, well, yes, but that was before Carol Fernandez outed me.

Then my dad wanted to know what outing was, so I

explained to him that outing is when somebody reveals your sexual orientation on national TV, or in the newspaper, or in some other large public forum. Only in this case, I explained, instead of my sexual orientation, my royal status had been revealed.

So then my dad said I couldn't go to a new school just because I'd been outed as being a princess. He said I have to stay at Albert Einstein, and Lars will go to class with me and protect me from reporters.

So then I asked him who'll drive him around, and he pointed to the new guy, Hans.

The new guy nodded to me in the rearview mirror and said, "Hi."

So then I said, "Lars is going to go with me everywhere I go?" Like how about if I just wanted to walk over to Lilly's? I mean, if Lilly and I were still friends. Which is certainly never going to happen now.

And my dad said, "Lars would go with you."

So basically, I am never going anywhere alone again.

This made me kind of mad. I sat in the backseat with red from a traffic light flashing down on my face, and I said, "Okay, well, that's it. I don't want to be a princess anymore. You can take back your one hundred dollars a day and send Grandmère back to France. I quit."

And my dad said, in this tired voice, "You can't quit, Mia. The article today closed the deal. Tomorrow your face will be in every newspaper in America—maybe even the world. Everyone will know that you are the princess Amelia of Genovia. And you cannot quit being who you are."

I guess it wasn't a very princessy thing to do, but I cried all the way to the Plaza. Lars gave me his handkerchief, which I thought was very nice of him.

My mom thinks the person who tipped off Carol Fernandez is Grandmère.

But I really can't believe Grandmère would do something like that—you know, give the *Post* the inside scoop on me. Especially when I'm so far behind in my princess lessons. You know? It's almost guaranteed that now I'm going to have to start acting like a princess—I mean, *really* acting like one—but Grandmère hasn't even gotten to all the really important stuff yet, the stuff like how to argue knowledgeably with virulent antiroyalists like Lilly. So far all Grandmère has taught me is how to sit; how to dress; how to use a fish fork; how to address senior members of the royal household staff; how to say thank you so much and no, I don't care for that, in seven languages; how to make a Sidecar; and some Marxist theory.

What good is any of THAT going to do me?

But my mom is convinced. Nothing will change her mind. My dad got really mad at her, but she still wouldn't budge. She says Grandmère is the one who tipped off Carol Fernandez and that all my dad has to do is ask her and he'll find out the truth.

My dad did ask her—not Grandmère. Mom. He asked her why she never bothered to consider that her boyfriend might be the one who spilled the beans to Carol Fernandez.

The minute he said it, I think my dad probably regretted it. Because my mom's eyes got the way they do when she's really mad—I mean *really* mad, like the time I told her about the guy in Washington Square Park who flashed his you-know-what at me and Lilly one day when we were filming for her show. Her eyes got narrower and narrower, until they were nothing more than little slits. Then, next thing I knew, she was putting on her coat and going out to kick some flasher butt.

Only she didn't put on her coat when my dad said that about Mr. Gianini. Instead, her eyes got very narrow, and her lips almost disappeared, she pressed them together so hard, and then she went, "Get . . . out," in a voice that kind of sounded like the poltergeist in that movie *Amityville Horror*.

But my dad wouldn't get out, even though technically the loft belongs to my mom (thank God Carol Fernandez didn't put the loft's address in the paper; and thank God my mom is so paranoid about Jesse Helms siccing the CIA on sociopolitical artists like herself, in order to yank their NEA grants, that she keeps our phone number unlisted; no reporters have discovered the loft, so we can at least order in Chinese without fear of hearing a story on *Extra* on how much the Princess Amelia likes moo shu vegetable).

Instead, my dad went, "Really, Helen. I think you're letting your dislike of my mother blind you to the real truth."

"The real truth?" my mom yelled. "The real truth, Phillipe, is that your mother is—"

At this point, I decided it might be best to retire to my room. I put my headphones on so I wouldn't have to listen to them fight. This is a trick I learned from watching kids on made-for-TV movies whose parents are divorcing. My favorite CD right now is the latest Britney Spears, which I know is really dorky, and I could never tell Lilly, but secretly I sort of want to be Britney Spears. Once I had a dream I *was* Britney, and I was performing in the auditorium at Albert Einstein, and I had this little pink minidress on, and Josh Richter complimented me on it right before I went onstage.

Isn't that an embarrassing thing to admit? The funny thing is, while I know I could never tell Lilly about that dream without her going all Freudian on me and telling me how the pink dress is a phallic symbol and being Britney signifies my low self-esteem or something, I know I could tell Tina Hakim Baba, and she would totally get into it and just want to know whether or not Josh was wearing leather pants.

I don't think I've ever mentioned this, but it's really hard to write with my new fake fingernails.

The more I think about it, the more I wonder whether or not Grandmère really is the one who tipped off Carol Fernandez. I mean, when I went to my princess lesson today I was still crying, and Grandmère was totally unsympathetic about it. She was all, "And these tears are because . . . ?" And when I told her, she just raised her painted-on eyebrows—she plucks hers all out and draws on new ones every day, which kind of defeats the purpose, if you ask me, but whatever—and went, *"C'est la vie,"* which means "Well, that's life" in French.

Only in life, I don't think a whole lot of girls get their faces plastered across the cover of the *Post*, unless they've won the lottery or had sex with the president or something. *I* didn't do anything except get born.

I don't think "that's life" at all. I think that sucks, is what I think.

Then Grandmère started talking about how she'd been fielding calls all day from representatives of the media, and how all these people want to interview me, like Leeza Gibbons and Barbara Walters and stuff, and she said I ought to have a press conference, and that she'd already talked to the Plaza people about it, and they'd set aside this special room with a podium and a pitcher of ice water and some potted palms and stuff.

I couldn't believe it! I was like, "Grandmère! I don't want to talk to Barbara Walters! God! Like I really want everyone knowing my business!"

And Grandmère said, all prissy, "Well, if you don't try to accommodate the media, they're just going to try to get the story any way they can, which means they'll keep showing up at your school. And at your friends' houses, and at your grocery store, and at the place where you rent those movie videos you like so much."

Grandmère doesn't believe in VCRs. She says if God meant for us to watch movies at home He wouldn't have invented coming attractions.

Then Grandmère wanted to know where my sense of civic duty was. She said it would greatly promote tourism in Genovia if I just went on *Dateline*.

I really want to do what's best for Genovia. I really do. But I also have to do what's best for Mia Thermopolis. And going on *Dateline* would definitely not be good for me.

But Grandmère seems really gung-ho on the whole promoting Genovia thing. So I sort of started to wonder if maybe, just maybe, my mom is right. Maybe Grandmère *did* talk to Carol Fernandez.

But would Grandmère do something like that?

Well. Yeah.

I just lifted up my headphones. They're still at it. Looks like it's going to be a long night.

Well, this morning my face was on the covers of the *Daily News* and *New York Newsday*. My picture was also in the Metro Section of *The New York Times*. They used my school photo, and let me tell you, my mom wasn't too happy about that, since that meant either somebody in our family, to whom she sent copies of that photo—which looks bad for Grandmère—or someone at Albert Einstein must have leaked it, which looks bad for Mr. Gianini. I wasn't too happy about it because my school photo was taken before Paolo fixed my hair and I look like one of those girls who are always going on TV to talk about their bad experience being in a cult or escaping from an abusive husband or something.

There were more reporters than ever in front of Albert Einstein when Hans pulled up in front of it this morning. I guess all the morning news shows needed something they could report live. Usually it's an overturned chicken truck on the Palisades Parkway or a crackhead holding his wife and kids hostage in Queens. But today it was me.

I had sort of anticipated that this might happen, and I was a little more prepared today than I was yesterday. So, in flagrant violation of my grandmother's fashion dictums, I wore my newly relaced combat boots (in case I had to kick anybody holding a microphone who got too close), and I also wore all of my Greenpeace and antifur buttons, so at least my celebrity status will be put to good use.

It was the same drill as the day before. Lars took me by the arm and the two of us sprinted through a sea of TV cameras and microphones into the school. As we ran, people shouted stuff at me like, "Amelia, do you intend to follow the example of Princess Diana and become the queen of people's hearts?" and "Amelia, who do you like better, Leonardo DiCaprio or Prince William?" and "Amelia, what are your feelings on the meat industry?"

They almost got me on that one. I started to turn around, but Lars dragged me on into the school.

HERE'S WHAT I NEED TO DO

1. Think of some way to get Lilly to like me again
2. Stop being such a wimp
3. Stop lying
   and/or
   Think of better lies
4. Stop being so dramatic
5. Start being more
   A. Independent
   B. Self-reliant
   C. Mature

6. Stop thinking about Josh Richter
7. Stop thinking about Michael Moscovitz
8. Get better grades
9. Achieve self-actualization

Today in Algebra Mr. Gianini was totally trying to teach us about the Cartesian plane, but nobody could pay attention because of all the news vans outside. People kept jumping up to lean out the windows and yell at the reporters: "You killed Princess Di! Bring back Princess Di!"

Mr. Gianini kept trying to bring people to order, but it was impossible. Lilly was getting all burned up because everyone was coming together against the reporters but no one had wanted to stand outside Ho's Deli and do her chant, which was "We oppose the racist Hos."

That's kind of harder to say than "You killed Princess Di! Bring back Princess Di!" so maybe that's why. Lilly's chant has too many big words.

So then Mr. Gianini had to have a talk with us about whether the media was really to blame for killing Princess Diana, or if maybe it was the fact that the guy driving the car she was in might have been drunk. And then somebody tried to say the driver hadn't been drunk, that he'd been poisoned and that it was all a plot by the British secret service, but Mr. Gianini said could we please come back to reality now.

And then Lana Weinberger wanted to know how long I'd known I was a princess, and I couldn't believe she was actually asking me a question without being snotty about it, and I was like, well, I don't know, a couple of weeks or something, and then Lana said if she found out she was a princess she would go straight to Disney World, and I said, no, you wouldn't, because you'd miss cheerleading practice, and then she said she didn't see why I didn't go to Disney World since I'm not even that involved in extracurricular activities, and then Lilly started in about the Disneyfication of America and how Walt Disney was actually a fascist, and then everybody started wondering if it was really true about his body being cryogenically frozen under the castle in Anaheim, and then Mr. Gianini was like, could we please return to the Cartesian plane?

Which is probably a safer plane to be on, if you think about it, than the one we live on, since there aren't any reporters there.

Cartesian coordinate system divides the plane into 4 parts called quadrants

So I was eating lunch with Tina Hakim Baba and Lars and Wahim, and Tina was telling me about how in Saudi Arabia, where her father comes from, girls have to wear this thing called a chadrah, which is like a huge blanket that covers them from head to foot with just a slit for them to see out of. It's supposed to protect them from the lustful eyes of men, but Tina says her cousins wear Gap jeans underneath their chadrahs, and as soon as there aren't any adults around they take their chadrahs off and hang out with boys just like we do.

Well, like we *would* do if any boys liked us.

I take that back. I forgot that Tina has a boy to hang out with, her Cultural Diversity date, Dave Farouq El-Abar.

Geez. What is *wrong* with me, anyway? How come no boys like *me*?

So Tina was telling me all about chadrahs when all of a sudden Lana Weinberger set her tray down next to ours.

I am not even kidding. *Lana Weinberger.*

I, of course, thought she was going to whip out the receipt for the Nutty Royaled sweater's dry cleaning or start shaking Tabasco sauce all over our salads or something, but instead she just went, all breezy, "You guys don't mind if we join you, do you?"

And then I saw this tray sliding over next to mine. It

was loaded down with two double cheeseburgers, large fries, two chocolate milks, a bowl of chili, a bag of Doritos, a salad with French dressing, a pack of Yodels, an apple, and a large Coke. When I looked up to see who could possibly be ingesting that many saturated fats, I saw Josh Richter pulling out the chair next to mine.

I am not even kidding. *Josh Richter.*

He went, "Hey," to me and sat down and started eating.

I looked at Tina, and Tina looked at me, and then both of us looked at our bodyguards. But they were busy arguing over whether rubber-tipped bullets really did hurt rioters or if it was better just to use hoses.

Tina and I looked back at Lana and Josh.

Really attractive people, like Lana and Josh, don't ever go anywhere alone. They always have this sort of entourage that follows them around. Lana's entourage consists of a bunch of other girls, most of whom are junior varsity cheerleaders like she is. They are all really pretty, with long hair and breasts and stuff, like Lana.

Josh's entourage consists of a bunch of senior boys who are all on the crew team with him. They are all really large and handsome, and they were all eating excessive amounts of animal by-products, just like Josh.

Josh's entourage put their trays down beside Josh's. Lana's entourage put their trays beside Lana's. And soon, our table, which had consisted only of two geeky girls and their bodyguards, was being graced by the most beautiful people in Albert Einstein—maybe even in all of Manhattan.

I got a good look at Lilly, and her eyes were bugging out the way they do when she sees something she thinks would make a good episode of her show.

"So," Lana said, all chatty-like, while she picked at her salad—no dressing, and only water on the side. "What are you up to this weekend, Mia? Are you going to the Cultural Diversity Dance?"

It was the first time she'd ever called me Mia and not Amelia.

"Uh," I said brilliantly. "Let me see . . ."

"Because Josh's parents are going away, and we were thinking about having a thing at his place on Saturday night, after the dance, and all. You should come."

"Huh," I said. "Well, I don't—"

"She should totally come," Lana said, stabbing at a cherry tomato with her fork. "Shouldn't she, Josh?"

Josh was shoveling chili into his mouth using Doritos instead of a spoon. "Sure," he said with his mouth full. "She should come."

"It's going to be so *cool*," Lana said. "Josh's place is like *great*. It's got six bedrooms. On Park Avenue. And there's a Jacuzzi in the master bedroom. Isn't there a Jacuzzi, Josh?"

Josh said, "Yeah, there's—"

Pierce, a member of Josh's entourage, and a six-foot-two-inch rower, interrupted. "Hey, Richter, remember after the last dance? When Bonham-Allen passed out in your mom's Jacuzzi? That was *rad*."

Lana giggled. "Oh, God! She chugged that whole bottle of Bailey's Irish Cream. Remember, Josh? She drank practically the whole thing herself—what a hog!—and then she wouldn't stop throwing up."

"Major vomitage," Pierce agreed.

"She had to have her stomach pumped," Lana said to Tina and me. "The paramedics said if Josh hadn't phoned them when he did she'd have died."

We all turned to look at Josh. He said, modestly, "It was *way* uncool."

Lana stopped giggling. "It was," she said, all solemn now that Josh Richter had declared the incident uncool.

I didn't know what I was supposed to say about that, so I just said, "Wow."

"So," Lana said. She ate a shred of lettuce and swished some water around in her mouth. "Are you coming, or not?"

"I'm sorry," I said. "I can't."

A lot of Lana's friends, who'd been talking among themselves, stopped talking and looked at me. Josh's friends, however, went right on eating.

"You *can't?*" Lana said, making this very astonished face.

"No," I said. "I can't."

"What do you mean, you *can't*?"

I thought about lying. I could have said something like, Lana, I can't go because I have to have dinner with the prime minister of Iceland. I could have said, I can't go because I have to go christen a cruise ship. There were all sorts of excuses I could have made up. But for once, for once in my stupid life, I went and told the truth.

"I can't go," I said, "because my mom wouldn't let me go to a party like that."

Oh, my God. Why did I say that? Why, why, why? I should have lied. I totally should have lied. Because how did I sound, saying something like that? Uh, like a total freak. Worse than a freak. A dork. A grade A nerd.

I don't know what compelled me to tell the truth in the first place. It wasn't even the *real* truth. I mean, it was *a* truth, but it wasn't the *real* reason I was saying no. I mean, it's true there was no way my mom was going to *let* me go to a party in a boy's apartment when his parents are out of town. Even with a bodyguard. But the real reason, of course, is that I wouldn't know how to *act* at a party like that. I mean, I've heard about these kinds of parties. There are like *whole rooms* reserved for people to go into to make out. We're talking major French kissing. Maybe even MORE than French kissing. Maybe even like above-the-waist touching. Maybe even below-the-waist touching. I don't know for sure, because no one I know has ever been to one of those parties. No one I know is popular enough to get invited.

Plus everybody drinks. But I don't drink, and I don't have anybody to make out with. So what would I *do* there?

Lana looked at me, and then she looked at her friends, and then she burst out laughing. Loud. I mean, REALLY loud.

Well, I guess I can't really blame her.

"Oh my God," Lana said when she had gotten over laughing so hard that she couldn't talk. "You can't be serious."

I knew right then Lana had just latched upon a whole new thing to torture me about. I didn't really care so much about me, but I felt bad for Tina Hakim Baba, who'd managed to keep such a low profile for so long. Suddenly, because of me, she was being sucked into the middle of the popular girl torture zone.

"Oh my God," Lana said. "Are you kidding me?"

"Um," I said. "No."

"Well, you're not supposed to tell her the *truth*," Lana said, all snotty again.

I didn't know what she was talking about.

"Your mom. *Nobody* tells their mom the *truth*. You tell her you're spending the night at a girlfriend's house. *Duh*."

Oh.

She meant lie. To my mom. Lana had obviously

never met my mom. *Nobody* lies to my mom. You just can't. Not about something like that. No way.

So I said, "Look, it's not like I don't appreciate being asked, and all, but I really don't think I can come. Besides, I don't even drink. . . ."

Okay, *that* was another big mistake.

Lana looked at me like I'd just said I'd never watched *Party of Five*, or something. She went: "You don't *drink*?"

I just looked at her. The truth is, at Miragnac I do drink. We drink wine with dinner every night. That's just what you do in France. You don't drink it for *fun*, though. You drink it because it goes with the food. It's supposed to make the foie gras taste better. I wouldn't know about that, since I don't eat foie gras, but I can tell you from experience that wine goes better with goat cheese than Dr Pepper does.

I certainly wouldn't chug a whole bottle of it, though, not even on a dare. Not even for Josh Richter.

So I just shrugged and went, "No. I try to be respectful of my body and not put a whole lot of toxins into it."

Lana snorted at that, but across from her—beside me—Josh Richter swallowed the mouthful of burger he was chewing and said, "I can respect that."

Lana's mouth dropped open. So, I'm sorry to say, did mine. Josh Richter respected something *I* had said? Are you *kidding* me?

But he looked perfectly serious. More than serious. He looked the way he had that day at Bigelows, like he could see into my soul with those electric blue eyes of his. . . . Like he already *had* seen into my soul. . . .

I guess Lana didn't notice her boyfriend looking into my soul, though. Because she said, "God, Josh. You drink more'n anybody else in this whole *school*."

Josh turned his head and looked at her with those hypnotic eyes. He said, without smiling, "Well, maybe I should quit, then."

Lana started laughing. She said, "Oh, right! That'll happen!"

Josh didn't laugh, though. He just went on looking at her.

That's when I started to get the heebie-jeebies. Josh just kept staring at Lana. I was glad he wasn't staring at *me* like that; those blue eyes of his are no joke.

I got up real fast and grabbed my tray. Tina, seeing what I was doing, did the same.

"Well," I said, "bye."

Then we booked out of there.

On the way to drop off our trays, Tina was like, "What was *that* all about?" and I said I didn't know. But I know one thing for sure:

For once, I'm kind of glad I'm not Lana Weinberger.

More Thursday, French

When I went to my locker after lunch to get my books for French, Josh was there. He was sort of leaning on his closed locker door, looking around. When he saw me coming, he straightened up and went, "Hey."

And then he smiled. A big smile that showed all of his white teeth. His perfectly straight white teeth. I had to look away, those teeth were so perfect and so blindingly white.

I said, "Hey," back. I was really embarrassed and all, since I had sort of seen him fighting with Lana a few minutes before. I figured he was probably waiting for her, and that the two of them would make up and probably French kiss all over the place, so I tried to work my combination as quickly as possible and get the heck out of there so I wouldn't have to watch.

But Josh started *talking* to me. He said, "I really agree with what you said in the caf just now. You know, about respecting your body and everything. I think that's really, you know, a cool attitude."

I could feel my face start to burn. It was sort of like I was on fire. I concentrated on not dropping anything as I moved books around in my locker. It's too bad my hair is so short now. I couldn't duck my head to hide the fact that I was blushing. "Huh," I said, real intelligently.

"So," Josh said, "are you going to the dance with anyone, or not?"

I dropped my Algebra book. It went skittering across the hall. I stooped down to pick it up.

"Um," I said, by way of answering his question.

I was down on my hands and knees, picking up old worksheets that had slid out of my Algebra book, when I saw these knees covered in gray flannel bend. Then Josh's face was right next to mine.

"Here," he said, and handed me my favorite pencil, the one with the feathery pom-pom on the end.

"Thanks," I said. Then I made the mistake of looking into his too-blue eyes.

"No," I said, real faintly, because that's how his eyes made me feel: faint. "I'm not going to the dance with anyone."

Then the bell rang.

Josh said, "Well, see you." And then he left.

I am still in shock.

Josh Richter *spoke* to me. He actually *spoke* to me. *Twice.*

For the first time in like a month, I don't care that I'm flunking Algebra. I don't care that my mom is dating one of my teachers. I don't care that I'm the heir to the throne of Genovia. I don't even care that my best friend and I aren't speaking.

I think Josh Richter might *like* me.

HOMEWORK

Algebra: ??? Can't remember!!!
English: ??? Ask Shameeka
World Civ: ??? Ask Lilly. Forgot. Can't ask Lilly.
She's not speaking to me.
G&T: none
French: ???
Biology: ???

God, just because a boy might like me, I completely
lose my head. I disgust myself.

Grandmère says: "Well, of course the boy likes you. What wouldn't he like? You are turning out very well, thanks to Paolo's handiwork and my tutelage."

Geez, Grandmère, thanks. Like it would be impossible for any guy to like me for *me*, and not because all of a sudden I'm a princess with a $200 haircut.

I think I sort of hate her.

I mean it. I know it's wrong to hate people, but I really do sort of hate my grandmother. At least, I strongly dislike her. I mean, besides the fact that she's totally vain and thinks only about herself, she's also kind of mean to people.

Like tonight, for instance:

Grandmère decided that for my lesson today we would go to dinner somewhere outside of the hotel so she could teach me how to deal with the press. Only there wasn't a whole lot of press around when we went outside, just some kid reporter from *Tiger Beat*, or something. I guess all the real reporters had gone home to get their dinner. (Plus it's no fun for the press to stalk you when you're ready for them. It's only when you least expect them that they come around. This is how they get their kicks, at least as far as I can figure out.)

Anyway, I was pretty happy about this, because who needs the press around, yelling questions and setting off flashbulbs in your face? Believe me, as it is, I see big purple splotches everywhere I go.

But then as I was getting into the car Hans had brought around, Grandmère said, "Wait one moment," and went back inside. I thought maybe she'd forgotten her tiara or something, but she came back out a minute later looking no different than before.

But then, when we pulled up in front of the restaurant, which was the Four Seasons, there were all these reporters there! At first I thought somebody important had to be inside, like Shaquille O'Neal or Madonna, but then they all started taking pictures of me and yelling "Princess Amelia, how does it feel to grow up in a single-parent household, then find out your mom's ex has three hundred million dollars?" and "Princess, what kind of running shoes do you wear?"

I totally forgot my whole fear of confrontation thing. I was mad. I turned to Grandmère in the car, and I said, "How did they know we were coming here?"

Grandmère just dug around in her purse for her cigarettes. "Now, what did I do with that lighter?" she asked.

"You called them, didn't you?" I was so mad, I could hardly even see straight. "You called and told them we were coming here."

"Don't be ridiculous," Grandmère said. "I had no time to call all these people."

"You didn't have to. You'd just have to call one, and

they'd all follow. Grandmère, *why?*"

Grandmère lit her cigarette. I hate when she smokes in the car. "This is an important part of being a royal, Amelia," she said between puffs. "You must learn to handle the press. Why are you taking on so?"

"You're the one who told all that stuff to Carol Fernandez." I said it totally calm.

"Of course I did," Grandmère said, with a kind of *So, what?* shrug.

"Grandma," I yelled. "How could you?"

She looked totally taken aback. She said, "Don't call me Grandma."

"Seriously," I yelled. "Dad thinks Mr. Gianini did it! He and Mom had this totally big fight about it. She said it was you, but he wouldn't believe her!"

Grandmère blew cigarette smoke out of her nostrils. "Phillipe," she said, "always was incredibly naïve."

"Well," I said, "I'm telling him. I'm telling him the truth."

Grandmère just waved a hand, as if to say *Whatever*.

"Seriously," I said. "I'm telling him. He's going to be really mad at you, Grandmère."

"He won't. You needed the practice, darling. That piece in the *Post* was only the beginning. Soon you'll be on the cover of *Vogue*, and then—"

"Grandmère!" I yelled. "I DO NOT WANT TO BE ON THE COVER OF *VOGUE*! DON'T YOU UNDERSTAND? I JUST WANT TO PASS THE

NINTH GRADE!"

Grandmère looked a little startled. "Well, all right, darling, all right. You needn't *shout*."

I don't know how much of that sank in, but after dinner I noticed the reporters had all gone home. So maybe she heard me.

When I got home, Mr. Gianini was here, AGAIN. I had to go into my room to call my dad. I said, "Dad, it was Grandma, not Mr. Gianini, who told Carol Fernandez everything," and he said, "I know," in this miserable way.

"You *know*?" I could hardly believe it. "You *know*, and you haven't said anything?"

He went, "Mia, your grandmother and I have a very complicated relationship."

He means he's scared of her. I guess I can't really blame him, considering the fact that she used to lock him in the dungeon and everything.

"Well," I said, "you could still apologize to Mom for what you said about Mr. Gianini."

He went, still sounding all miserable, "I know."

So I said, "Well? Are you going to?"

And he said, "Mia . . . " Only now he sounded all exasperated. I figured I'd done enough good deeds for one day, and hung up.

After that, I sat around while Mr. Gianini helped me with my homework. I was too distracted by Josh Richter's talking to me today to pay attention while

Michael was trying to help me in G and T.

I guess I can sort of see how my mom likes Mr. G. He's okay to just hang out with, you know, like in front of the TV. He doesn't hog the remote, like some of my mom's past boyfriends. And he doesn't seem to care about sports at all.

About a half hour before I went to bed, my dad called back and asked to speak to my mother. She went into the room to talk to him, and when she came out again she looked all smug, in an I-told-you-so sort of way.

I wish I could tell Lilly about Josh Richter talking to me.

OH MY GOD!!!
JOSH AND LANA BROKE UP!!!!

I am not even kidding. It's all over school. Josh broke up with her last night after crew practice. They were having dinner together at the Hard Rock Cafe, and he asked for his class ring back!!! Lana was completely humiliated under the pointy cone bra Gaultier made for Madonna!

I wouldn't wish that on my worst enemy.

Lana wasn't hanging around Josh's locker this morning, like usual. And then when I saw her in Algebra, her eyes were all red and squinty, and her hair looked like it hadn't been brushed, let alone washed, and her thigh-highs had come unglued and were all baggy around her knees. I never thought I'd see Lana Weinberger looking like a mess!!! Before class started, she was on her cell phone with Bergdorf's, trying to convince them to take her Cultural Diversity Dance dress back even though she'd already removed the tags. Then, during class, she sat there with a big black marker crossing out *"Mrs. Josh Richter"* from where she'd written it all over her book covers.

It was so depressing. I could hardly factor my integers, I was so distracted.

I WISH I WERE

1. A size 36 double D
2. Good at math
3. A member of a world-famous rock band
4. Still friends with Lilly Moscovitz
5. Josh Richter's new girlfriend

You will not even believe what just happened. I was putting my Algebra book away in my locker, and Josh Richter was there getting his Trig notes, and he goes, in this totally casual way, "Hey, Mia, who you going to the dance with tomorrow?"

Needless to say, the fact that he actually spoke to me at all practically caused me to pass out. And then the fact that he was actually saying something that sounded like it might be a prelude to asking me out—well, I nearly threw up. I mean it. I felt really sick, but in a good way.

I think.

Somehow, I managed to stammer out, "Uh, no one," and he goes, and I kid you not:

"Well, why don't we go together?"

OH MY GOD!!!!! JOSH RICHTER ASKED ME OUT!!!!!

I was so shocked I couldn't say anything at all for like a minute. I thought I was going to hyperventilate, like I did the time I saw that documentary about how cows become hamburgers. I could only stand there and look up at him. (He's so tall!)

Then a funny thing happened. This tiny part of my brain—the only part that wasn't completely stunned by his asking me out—went: He's only asking you out because you're the princess of Genovia.

Seriously. That's what I thought, for just a second.

Then this other part of my brain, a much bigger part, went: SO WHAT???

I mean, maybe he asked me to the dance because he respects me as a human being and wants to get to know me better and maybe, just maybe, likes me, sort of.

It could happen.

So the part of my brain that was rationalizing all this made me go, all nonchalantly, "Yeah, okay. That might be fun."

Then Josh said a bunch of stuff about how he'd pick me up and we'd have dinner beforehand or something. But I barely heard him. Because inside my head, this voice was going:

Josh Richter just asked you out. Josh Richter just asked YOU out. JOSH RICHTER JUST ASKED YOU OUT!!!!

I think I must have died and gone to heaven. Because it had happened. It had finally happened: Josh Richter had finally looked into my soul. He had looked into my soul, and had seen the real me, the one beneath the flat chest. AND THEN HE'D ASKED ME OUT.

Then the bell rang, and Josh went away, and I just kept standing there until Lars poked me in the arm.

I don't know what Lars's problem is. I *know* he's not my personal secretary.

But thank God he was there, or I'd never have

known Josh was picking me up tomorrow night at seven. I'm going to have to learn not to be so shocked the next time he asks me out, or I'll never get the hang of this dating thing.

THINGS TO DO (I THINK, NEVER HAVING BEEN ON A DATE BEFORE, I AM NOT EXACTLY SURE WHAT TO DO)

1. Get a dress
2. Get hair done
3. Get nails redone (stop biting fake ones off)

Okay, so I don't know who Lilly Moscovitz thinks she is. First she stops talking to me. Then, when she finally does deign to speak to me, it's only to criticize me some more. What right has she got, I ask you, to dump all over my Cultural Diversity Dance date? I mean, *she's* going with Boris Pelkowski. *Boris Pelkowski.* Yeah, he might be a musical genius and all, but he's still *Boris Pelkowski.*

Lilly goes: "Well, at least I know Boris isn't on the rebound."

Excuse me. Josh Richter is *not* on the rebound. He and Lana had been broken up for sixteen whole hours before he asked me out.

Lilly goes: "Plus Boris doesn't do *drugs.*"

I swear, for someone so smart, Lilly sure does go for the whole rumor and innuendo thing in a major way. I asked her if she'd ever *seen* Josh do drugs, and she looked at me all sarcastically.

But really, if you think about it, there isn't any *proof* Josh does drugs. He definitely hangs out with people who do drugs, but hey, Tina Hakim Baba hangs out with a princess, and that doesn't make *her* one.

Lilly didn't like that argument, though. She went: "You're overrationalizing. Whenever you overrationalize, Mia, I know you're worried."

I am *not* worried. I am going to the biggest dance of

the fall semester with the cutest, most sensitive boy in school, and nothing anyone can do or say will make me feel bad about that.

Except that it does kind of make me feel weird, seeing Lana looking so sad and Josh looking like he doesn't care at all. Today at lunch, he and his entourage sat with Tina and me, and Lana and her entourage sat back with the other cheerleaders. It was just so *strange*. Plus neither Josh nor any of his friends talked to me or to Tina. They just talked to each other. Which didn't bother Tina any, but it kind of bothered me. Especially since Lana kept trying so hard not to look over at our table.

Tina didn't say anything bad about Josh when I told her the news. She just got very excited and said tonight, when I spend the night, we can try on different outfits and experiment with our hair to see what will look best for tomorrow night. Well, I have no hair to experiment with, but we can experiment with her hair. Actually, Tina's almost more excited than I am. She is a much more supportive friend than Lilly, who went, all sarcastically, when she heard: "Where's he taking you to dinner? The Harley-Davidson Cafe?"

I said, "No," very sarcastically. "Tavern on the Green."

Lilly went, "Oh, how imaginative."

I suppose superartsy Boris is taking *her* somewhere in the Village.

Then Michael, who had been pretty quiet (for him) all through class, looked at Lars and went, "You're going, too, right?"

And Lars went, "Oh, yes." And the two of them looked at each other in that infuriating way guys look at each other sometimes, like they have this secret. You know in sixth grade, when they made all of us girls go into this other room and watch a video about getting our periods and stuff? I bet while we were gone, the boys were watching a video about how to look at each other in that infuriating way.

Or maybe a cartoon or something.

But now that I think of it, Josh *is* kind of dissing Lana. I mean, he probably shouldn't have asked out another girl so soon after breaking up with her—at least, not to something he was going to go to with her. Know what I mean? I kind of feel bad about the whole thing.

But not bad enough not to go.

FROM NOW ON I WILL

1. Be nicer to everyone, even Lana Weinberger.
2. Never ever bite my fingernails, even the fake ones.
3. Write faithfully in this journal every day.

4. Stop watching old Baywatch reruns and use my time wisely, like to study Algebra, or maybe improve the environment, or something.

Friday Night

Abbreviated lesson with Grandmère today because of my spending the night at Tina's. Grandmère had pretty much gotten over my yelling at her yesterday about the press. She was totally into helping me figure out what I'm going to wear tomorrow night, just like I knew she would. She got on the phone with Chanel and set up an appointment for tomorrow to pick something out. It will have to be a rush job, and will cost a fortune, but she says she doesn't care. It will be my first formal event as a representative of Genovia, and I have to "sparkle" (her word, not mine).

I pointed out to her that it was a school dance, not an inauguration ball or anything, and that it wasn't even a prom, just a stupid dance to celebrate the diversity of the various racial and cultural groups that attend Albert Einstein High School. But Grandmère went ape anyway, and kept on worrying there wouldn't be time to dye shoes to match my gown.

There's a lot of stuff about being a girl I never realized. Like having your shoes match your gown. I didn't know that was so important.

But Tina Hakim Baba sure knows. You should see her room. She must have every women's magazine ever printed. They are in order on shelves all around her room, which, by the way, is huge and pink, much like the rest of her apartment, which takes up the entire top floor of her building. You hit PH on the elevator buttons, and the elevator opens in the Hakim Babas' marble foyer, which really does have a fountain, only you're not supposed to throw pennies in it, I found out.

And then there's just room after room after room. They have a maid, a cook, a nanny, and a driver, all of whom live in. So you can imagine how many rooms there are, on top of the fact that Tina has three little sisters and a baby brother, and all of *them* have their own rooms, too.

Tina's room has its own 37-inch TV with a Sony PlayStation. I can see now that I have been living a life of monastic simplicity compared to Tina.

Some people have all the luck.

Anyway, Tina is a lot different at home than she is at school. At home, she's totally bubbly and outgoing. Her parents are pretty nice, too. Mr. Hakim Baba is really funny. He had a heart attack last year and isn't allowed to eat practically anything but vegetables and rice. He has to lose twenty more pounds. He kept pinching my arm and going, "How do you stay so skinny?" I told him about my strict vegetarianism, and he went, "Oh," and shuddered really hard. The Hakim Babas' cook has orders to prepare only vegetarian meals, which was good for me. We had couscous and vegetable goulash. It was all quite delicious.

Mrs. Hakim Baba is beautiful, but in a different way than my mom. Mrs. Hakim Baba is British and very blond. I think she's pretty bored, living here in America and not having a job and all. Mrs. Hakim Baba used to be a model, but she quit when she got married. Now she doesn't get to meet all the interesting people she used to meet when she was modeling. She once stayed in the same hotel as Prince Charles and Princess Diana. She says they slept in separate bedrooms. And that was on their honeymoon!

No wonder things didn't work out between them.

Mrs. Hakim Baba is as tall as me, which makes her about five inches taller than Mr. Hakim Baba. But I don't think Mr. Hakim Baba minds.

Tina's little sisters and brother are really cute. After we messed around with the fashion magazines, looking up hairstyles, we tried some of them out on Tina's sisters. They looked pretty funny. Then we put butterfly clips in Tina's little brother's hair and gave him a French manicure like mine, and he got very excited and changed into his Batman suit and ran around the apartment, screaming. I thought it was cute, but Mr. and Mrs. Hakim Baba didn't think so. They made the nanny put little Bobby Hakim Baba to bed right after dinner.

Then Tina showed me her dress for tomorrow. It's a Nicole Miller. It's so pretty, like sea foam. Tina Hakim Baba looks much more like a princess than I ever could.

Then it was time for *Lilly Tells It Like It Is*, which comes on on Friday nights at nine. This was the episode dedicated to exposing the unjust racism at Ho's Deli. It was filmed before Lilly called off the boycott due to lack of interest. It was a very hard-hitting piece of television news journalism, and I can say that without bragging, since I wasn't involved in its creation. If *Lilly Tells It Like It Is* ever went network, I bet it would be as highly rated as *60 Minutes*.

At the end, Lilly came on and did a segment she must have shot the night before, with a tripod in her bedroom. She sat on her bed and said that racism is a powerful force of evil that all of us must work to combat. She said that even though paying five cents more for a bag of gingko biloba rings might not seem like much to some of us, victims of real racism, like the Armenians and the Rwandans and the Ugandans and the Bosnians, would recognize that that five cents was only the first step on the road to genocide. Lilly went on to say that because of her daring stand against the Hos there was a little bit more justice on the side of right today.

I don't know about that, but I did sort of start to miss her when she waggled her feet, in their furry bear claw slippers, into the camera as a tribute to Norman. Tina is a fun friend and everything, but I've known Lilly since kindergarten. It's kind of hard to forget that.

We stayed up really late reading Tina's teenage love novels. I swear, there wasn't a single one where the boy broke up with a snotty girl and started going out with the heroine right away. Usually he waited a tactful amount of time, like a summer or at least a weekend, before asking her out. The only ones with a guy who started going out with the heroine right away turned out to be ones where the guy was just using the girl to get revenge or something.

But then Tina said even though she loves reading those books, she never takes them as a guide to real life. Because how many times in real life does anybody ever get amnesia? And when do cute young European terrorists ever take anybody hostage in the girls' locker room? And if they did, wouldn't it be on the day when you're wearing your worst underwear, the kind with the holes and loose elastic, and a bra that doesn't match, and not a pink silk camisole and tap pants, like the heroine of that particular book?

She has a point.

Tina's turning out the light now, because she's tired. I'm glad. It's been a long day.

When I got home, the first thing I did was check to make sure Josh hadn't called to cancel.

He hadn't.

Mr. Gianini was there, though (of course). This time he had pants on, thank God. When he heard me ask my mom if a boy named Josh had called, he was all, "You don't mean Josh Richter, do you?"

I got kind of mad, because he sounded . . . I don't know. Shocked or something.

I said, "Yes, I mean Josh Richter. He and I are going to the Cultural Diversity Dance tonight."

Mr. Gianini raised his eyebrows. "What about that Weinberger girl?"

It kind of sucks to have a parent who's dating a teacher in your school. I went, "They broke up."

My mom was watching us pretty closely, which is unusual for her, since most of the time she's in her own world. She went, "Who's Josh Richter?"

And I went, "Only the cutest, most sensitive boy in school."

Mr. Gianini snorted and said, "Well, most popular, anyway."

To which my mom replied, with a lot of surprise, "And he asked *Mia* to the dance?"

Needless to say, this was not very flattering. When your own mother knows it's weird for the cutest, most popular boy in school to ask you to the dance, you know you're in trouble.

"Yes," I said, all defensively.

"I don't like this," Mr. Gianini said. And when my mom asked him why, he said, "Because I know Josh Richter."

My mom went, "Uh oh. I don't like the sound of that," and before I could say anything in Josh's defense, Mr. Gianini went, "That boy is going one hundred miles per hour," which doesn't even make any sense.

At least it didn't until my mom pointed out that since I'm only going five miles per hour (FIVE!) she was going to have to consult my father "about this."

Hello? Consult him about what? What am I, a car with a faulty fan belt? What's this five-miles-per-hour stuff?

"He's fast, Mia," Mr. Gianini translated.

Fast? FAST? What is this, the fifties? Josh Richter is a rebel without a cause all of a sudden?

My mom went, as she was dialing my dad's phone number over at the Plaza, "You're just a freshman. You shouldn't be going out with seniors anyway."

How unfair is THAT? I finally get a date, and all of a sudden my parents turn into Mike and Carol Brady? I mean, come on!

So I was standing there, listening to my mom and dad over the speakerphone go on about how they both think I'm too young to date and that I SHOULDN'T date, since this has been a very confusing time for me, what with finding out I'm a princess and all. They were planning out the rest of my life for me (no dating until I'm eighteen, all-girls dorm when I get to college, etc.) when the buzzer to the loft went off, and Mr. G went to answer it. When he asked who it was, this all-too-familiar voice went, "This is Clarisse Marie Grimaldi Renaldo. Who is *this*?"

Across the room, my mom nearly dropped the phone. It was Grandmère. Grandmère had come to the loft!

I never in my life thought I'd be grateful to Grandmère for something. I never thought I'd be glad to see her. But when she showed up at the loft to take me shopping for my dress, I could have kissed her—on both cheeks, even—I really could have. Because when I met her at the door, I was like, "Grandmère, they won't let me go!"

I forgot Grandmère had never even been to the loft before. I forgot Mr. Gianini was there. All I could think about was the fact that my parents were trying to low-ball me about Josh. Grandmère would take care of it, I knew.

And boy, did she ever.

Grandmère came bursting in, giving Mr. Gianini a very dirty look—"This is *he*?" she stopped long enough to ask, and when I said yes, she made this sniffing sound and walked right by him—and heard Dad on the speakerphone. She shouted, "Give me that phone," at my mother, who looked like a kid who'd just gotten caught jumping a turnstile by the Transit Authority.

"Mother?" my dad's voice shouted over the speakerphone. You could tell he was in almost as much shock as Mom. "Is that you? What are *you* doing there?"

For someone who claims to have no use for modern technology, Grandmère sure knew how to work that speakerphone. She took Dad right off it, snatched the receiver out of my mother's hand, and went, "Listen here, Phillipe," into it. "Your daughter is going to the dance with her beau. I traveled fifty-seven blocks by limo to take her shopping for a new dress, and if you think I'm not going to watch her dance in it, then you can just—"

Then my grandmother used some pretty strong language. Only since she said it all in French, only my dad and I understood. My mom and Mr. Gianini just stood there. My mom looked mad. Mr. G looked nervous.

After my grandmother had finished telling my dad just where he could get off, she slammed the phone down, then looked around the loft. Let's just say Grandmère has never been one for hiding her feelings, so I wasn't too surprised when the next thing she said was, "*This* is where the princess of Genovia is being brought up? In this . . . *warehouse?*"

Well, if she had lit a firecracker under my mom, she couldn't have made her madder.

"Now look here, Clarisse," my mother said, stomping around in her Birkenstocks. "Don't you dare try to tell me how to raise my child! Phillipe and I have already decided she isn't going out with this boy. You can't just come in here and—"

"Amelia," my grandmother said, "go and get your coat."

I went. When I got back, my mom's face was really red, and Mr. Gianini was looking at the floor. But neither of them said anything as Grandmère and I left the loft.

Once we were outside, I was so excited I could hardly stand it. "Grandmère!" I yelled. "What'd you *say* to them? What'd you say to convince them to let me go?"

But Grandmère just laughed in this scary way and said, "I have my ways."

Boy, did I ever not hate her then.

More Saturday

Well, I'm sitting here in my new dress, my new shoes, my new nails, and my new panty hose, with my newly waxed legs and underarms, my newly touched-up hair, my professionally made-up face, and it's seven o'clock, and there's no sign of Josh, and I'm wondering if maybe this whole thing was a joke, like in the movie *Carrie*, which is too scary for me to watch but Michael Moscovitz rented it once, and then he told Lilly and me what it was about: This homely girl gets asked to a dance by the most popular boy in school just so he and his popular friends can pour pig blood on her. Only he doesn't know Carrie has psychic powers, and at the end of the night she kills everyone in the whole town, including Steven Spielberg's first wife and the mom from *Eight Is Enough*.

The problem is, of course, I don't have psychic powers, so if it turns out that Josh and his friends pour pig blood on me I won't be able to kill them all. I mean, unless I call in the Genovian national guard or something. But that would be difficult, since Genovia doesn't have an air force or navy, so how would the guards get here? They'd have to fly commercially, and it costs A LOT to buy tickets at the last minute. I doubt my dad would approve such an exorbitant expenditure of government funds—especially for what he'd be bound to consider a frivolous reason.

But if Josh Richter stands me up, I can assure you, I will *not* have a frivolous reaction. I got my LEGS waxed for him. Okay? And if you think that doesn't hurt, think about having your UNDERARMS waxed, which I also had done for him. Okay? That waxing stuff HURTS. I practically started to cry, it hurt so bad. So don't be telling ME we can't call out the Genovian national guard if I get stood up.

I know my dad thinks Josh has stood me up. He's sitting at the kitchen table right now, pretending to read *TV Guide*. But I see him sneaking peeks at his watch all the time. Mom, too. Only she never wears a watch, so she keeps sneaking peeks at the blinking-eye cat clock on the wall.

Lars is here, too. He isn't checking the clock, though. He keeps checking his ammunition clip to make sure he has enough bullets. I suppose my dad told him to shoot Josh if he makes a move on me.

Oh, yes. My dad said I can go out with Josh, but only if Lars goes, too. This is no big thing since I always expected Lars would go, anyway. But I pretended to be all mad about it so my dad wouldn't think I was getting off too easy. I mean, HE's in BIG trouble with Grandmère. She told me while I was being fitted for my dress that my dad has always had a problem with commitment and that the reason he doesn't want me to go out with Josh is that he can't stand to see me dumped the way my dad has dumped countless models all over the world.

God! Assume the worst, why don't you, Dad.

Josh can't dump me. He's never even been out with me yet.

And if he doesn't show up soon, well, all I can say is HIS LOSS. I look better than I have ever looked in my whole entire life. Old Coco Chanel really outdid herself; my dress is HOT, pale, pale blue silk, all scrunched up on top like an accordion, so my being flat-chested doesn't even show, then straight and skinny the rest of the way down, all the way to my matching pale, pale blue silk high heels. I think I kind of resemble an icicle, but according to the ladies at Chanel, this is the look of the new millennium. Icicles are *in*.

The only problem is I can't pet Fat Louie or I'll get orange cat hair on myself. I should have got one of those masking tape roller thingies last time I was at Rite Aid, but I forgot. Anyway, he's sitting beside me on the futon, looking all sad because I won't pet him. I picked up all my socks, just in case he got it into his head to punish me or something by eating one.

My dad just looked at his watch and went, "Hmm. Seven-fifteen. I can't say much for this boy's promptness."

I tried to remain calm. "I'm sure there's a lot of traffic," I said, in as princessy a voice as I could.

"I'm sure," said my dad. He didn't sound very sad, though. "Well, Mia, we can still make it to *Beauty and the Beast*, if you want to go. I'm sure I can get—"

"Dad!" I was horrified. "I am NOT going to *Beauty and the Beast* with you tonight."

Now he sounded sad. "But you used to love *Beauty and the Beast*. . . ."

THANK GOD the intercom just rang. It's him. My mom just buzzed him up. The other stipulation, before my dad would let me go, is that besides Lars going, Josh has to meet both my parents—and probably submit proof of ID, though I'm not sure Dad's thought of that yet.

I'm going to have to leave this book here, because there's no room for it in my "clutch," which is what my skinny, flat purse is called.

Oh my God, my hands are sweating so hard! I should have listened when Grandmère suggested those elbow-length gloves—

Saturday Night, Ladies' Room, Tavern on the Green

Okay, so I lied. I brought this book anyway. I made Lars carry it. Well, it's not like he doesn't have room in that briefcase he carries around. I know it's filled with silencers and grenades and stuff, but I knew he could fit one measly journal into it.

And I was right.

So I'm in the bathroom at the Tavern on the Green. The ladies' room here isn't as nice as the one at the Plaza. There isn't a little stool to sit on in my stall, so I'm sitting on the toilet with the lid down. I can see a lot of fat ladies' feet moving around outside my stall door. There are a whole lot of fat ladies here, mostly for this wedding between a very Italian-looking dark-haired girl who needs a good eyebrow waxing and a skinny red-headed boy named Fergus. Fergus gave me the old eye-ball when I walked into the dining room. I am not kidding. My first married man, even if he has only been married about an hour and looks my age. This dress is the BOMB!

Dinner's not so great as I thought it would be, though. I mean, I know from Grandmère which fork to use and all that, and to tilt my soup bowl away from me, but that's not it.

It's Josh.

Don't get me wrong. He looks totally hot in his tux.

He told me he owns it. Last year, he escorted his girl-friend before Lana to all the debutante events in the city, his girlfriend before Lana having been related to the guy who invented those plastic bags you put vegetables in when you go to the grocery store. Only his were the first to say OPEN HERE so you knew which end was the one you were supposed to try to open. Those two little words earned the guy half a billion dollars, Josh says.

I don't know why he told me this. Am I supposed to be impressed by something his ex-girlfriend's dad did? He isn't acting very sensitive, to tell you the truth.

Still, he was really good with my parents. He came in, gave me a corsage (tiny white roses tied together with pink ribbon, totally gorgeous; it must have cost him ten dollars *at least*—I couldn't help thinking, though, that he'd originally picked it out for another girl, with a different color dress), and shook my dad's hand. He said, "It's a pleasure to meet you, Your Highness," which made my mom start laughing really loud. She can be so embarrassing sometimes.

Then he turned to my mom and said, "You're Mia's mother? Oh my gosh, I thought you must be her college-age sister," which is a totally foolish thing to say, but my mom actually fell for it, I think. She BLUSHED as he was shaking her hand. I guess I am not the only Thermopolis woman to fall under the spell of Josh Richter's blue eyes.

Then my dad cleared his throat and started asking

Josh a whole lot of questions about what kind of car he was driving (his dad's BMW), where we're going (duh), and what time we would be back (in time for breakfast, Josh said). My dad didn't like that, though, and Josh said, "What time would you like her back, sir?"

SIR! Josh Richter called my dad SIR!

And my dad looked at Lars and said, "One o'clock at the latest," which I thought was pretty decent of him, since my normal curfew is eleven on weekends. Of course, considering that Lars was going to be there, and there wasn't anything that could actually happen to me, it was kind of bogus that I couldn't stay out as late as I wanted, but Grandmère told me a princess should always be prepared to compromise, so I didn't say anything.

Then my dad asked Josh some more questions, like where was he going to college in the fall (he hasn't decided yet, but he's applying to all the Ivy Leagues) and what does he plan on studying (business), and then my mom asked him what was wrong with a liberal arts education, and Josh said he was really looking for a degree that would guarantee him a minimum salary of eighty thousand a year, to which my mom replied that there are more important things than money, and then I said, "Gosh, look at the time," and grabbed Josh and headed out the door.

Josh and Lars and I went down to Josh's dad's car, and Josh held the door to the front seat open for me, and then Lars said why didn't he drive so Josh and I could sit in the back and get to know each other. I thought this was way nice of Lars, but when Josh and I got in the back, we didn't have a whole lot to say to each other. I mean, Josh was like, "You look really nice in that dress," and I said I liked his tux and thanked him for my corsage. And then we didn't say anything for like twenty blocks.

I am not even kidding. I was so embarrassed! I mean, I don't hang around with boys that much, but I've never had that problem with the ones I HAVE hung around with. I mean, Michael Moscovitz practically never shuts up. I couldn't understand why Josh wasn't SAYING anything. I thought about asking him who he'd rather spend eternity with if it was the end of the world and he had to choose, Winona Ryder or Nicole Kidman, but I didn't feel like I knew him well enough. . . .

But finally Josh broke the silence by asking if it was true my mom was dating Mr. Gianini. Well, I should have expected *that* to get around. Maybe not as fast as my being a princess, but it had gotten around, all right.

So I said, yes, it was true, and then Josh wanted to know what that was like.

But then for some reason I couldn't tell him about seeing Mr. G in his underwear at my kitchen table. It just didn't seem . . . I don't know. I just couldn't tell him. Isn't that funny? I had told Michael Moscovitz without even having been asked. But I couldn't tell Josh, even though he had looked into my soul and everything. Weird, huh?

Then after like a zillion more blocks of silence we pulled up in front of the restaurant, and Lars surrendered the car to the valet and Josh and I went in (Lars promised he wouldn't eat with us; he said he'd just stand by the door and look at everybody who arrived in a mean way, like Arnold Schwarzenegger), and it turned out all of Josh's entourage was meeting us here, which I didn't know but was kind of relieved to see. I mean, I'd sort of been dreading sitting there for another hour or so with nothing to say. . . .

But thank God, all the guys on the crew team were at this big long table with their cheerleader girlfriends, and at the head of this table were these two empty places, one for Josh and one for me.

I have to say, everyone has been pretty nice. The girls all complimented me on my dress and asked me questions about being a princess, like how weird was it to wake up and see your picture on the front of the *Post*, and do you ever wear a crown, and stuff like that. They're all much older than me—some of them are seniors—so they're pretty mature. None of them have made any comments about how I have no chest or anything, like Lana would have if she'd been here.

But then, if Lana were here I wouldn't be.

The thing that most surprised me is that Josh

ordered champagne, and nobody even questioned his ID, which, of course, was totally fake. The table's been through three bottles already, and Josh just keeps ordering more, since his dad gave him his platinum American Express card for the occasion. I just don't get it. Can't the waiters tell he's only eighteen and that most of his guests are even younger than that?

And how can Josh sit there and drink so much? What if Lars hadn't been here to drive? Josh would be driving his dad's BMW half sloshed. How irresponsible can you get? And Josh is class valedictorian!

And then, without even asking me, Josh ordered dinner for the whole table: filet mignon for everyone. I guess that's very nice and all, but I won't eat meat, not even for the most sensitive boy in the world.

And he hasn't even noticed I haven't touched my food! I totally had to fill up on salad and bread rolls to keep from starving to death.

Maybe I could sneak out of here and get Lars to pick up a veggie wrap for me from Emerald Planet.

And the funny thing is, the more champagne Josh has to drink, the more he keeps on touching me. Like he keeps on putting his hand on my leg under the table. At first I thought it was a mistake, but he's done it four times now. The last time, he squeezed!

I don't think he's drunk, exactly, but he's certainly friendlier than he was in the car on the way up. Maybe he's just feeling less inhibited, with Lars not hovering around, two feet away.

Well, I guess I should go back out there. I just wish Josh had told me we were meeting his friends. Then maybe I could have invited Tina Hakim Baba and her date—or even Lilly and Boris. Then at least I'd have someone fun to talk to.

Oh, well. Here goes nothing.

Why?

Why??

Why???

I can't even believe this is happening. I can't believe it's happening to ME!

WHY? WHY ME? WHY IS IT ALWAYS ME these things have to happen to????

I'm trying to remember what Grandmère told me about how to act under duress. Because I am definitely under duress. I keep trying to breathe in through my nose, out through my mouth, like Grandmère said. In through my nose, out through my mouth. In through my nose, out through my—

HOW COULD HE DO THIS TO ME???? HOW, HOW, HOW?????!!!

I could rip his stupid face off, I really could. I mean, who does he think he is? Do you know what he did? Do you know what he did? Well, let me tell you what he did.

After polishing off NINE bottles of champagne—that's practically one bottle per person, except I only had a couple of sips, so somebody drank my bottle as well as his—Josh and his friends finally decided it was time to go to the dance. Oh, gee, let me see, the dance had only started an HOUR earlier. It was only about TIME we left.

So we go and wait for the valet to bring the car around, and I was thinking maybe everything would be all right, since while we were waiting Josh had his arm around my shoulders, which was really nice, since my dress is sleeveless, and even though I have a wrap it's just this shimmery see-through veil thing. So I'm appreciative of this arm, since it's keeping me warm. It's a nice arm, really, very muscular from all that rowing. The only problem is, Josh doesn't smell that good, not a bit like Michael Moscovitz, who always smells like soap. No, I think Josh must have taken a bath in Drakkar Noir, which in large doses actually smells pretty vile. I could hardly breathe, but whatever. In spite of that, I'm thinking, okay, things aren't so bad. Yes, he didn't respect my rights as a vegetarian, but you know, everybody makes mistakes. We'll go to the dance and he'll look into my soul again with those electric blue eyes and everything will be all right.

Boy, was I ever wrong.

First of all, we can barely pull up to the school, there's so much traffic. At first I couldn't figure it out. Yes, it was Saturday night, but there shouldn't be THAT much traffic in front of Albert Einstein's, right? I mean, it's just a school dance. Most kids in New York City don't even have access to cars, right? We're probably like the only people who go to Albert Einstein's who drove.

And then I realize why there's so much congestion.

There are news vans parked all over the place. They're shining these big bright lights all over the steps to Albert Einstein's. There are reporters swarming around all over the place, smoking cigarettes, talking on cell phones, waiting.

Waiting for what?

Waiting for me, it turns out.

As soon as Lars saw the lights, he started to swear very colorfully in some language that wasn't English or French. But you could tell they were swear words by his voice. I leaned forward and was like, "How could they have known? How could they have known? Could Grandmère have told them?"

But you know, I really don't think Grandmère would have done this. I really don't. Not after our talk. I laid it on the line for Grandmère. I came down on her like a New York cop on a game of three-card monte. Grandmère would not, I'm sure, EVER call the press on me again, without my permission.

But there they all were, and SOMEBODY called them, all right, and if it wasn't Grandmère, then who was it?

Josh was totally unconcerned by all the lights and cameras and everything. He goes, "So what? You ought to be used to it by now."

Oh, right. Let me tell you how used to it I am by now. So used to it that the thought of getting out of that car, even with the arm of the cutest boy in the school around me, made me feel like I was going to barf up all of that salad and bread.

"Come on," Josh said. "You and I can make a run for it while Lars goes and parks the car."

Lars totally did not like that idea. He went, "I think not. *You* will park the car, and the princess and *I* will make a run for it."

But Josh was already opening his door. He had hold of my hand. He said, "Come on. You only live once," and started dragging me out of the car.

And like the really stupid chump that I am, I let him.

That's right. I let him drag me out of the car. Because his hand felt so nice over mine, so big and protective, so warm and secure, I thought, Oh, what could happen? So a bunch of flashbulbs will go off. So what? We'll just make a run for it, like he said. Everything will be fine.

So I said to Lars, "That's okay, Lars. You park the car. Josh and I'll go on inside."

Lars said, "No, Princess, wait—"

Which were the last words I heard out of him—for a while, anyway—since by that time Josh and I were out of the car and he had slammed the door shut behind us.

And then, instantly, the press was on us, everyone throwing down their cigarettes and pulling the lens caps off their cameras, yelling, "It's her! It's her!"

And then Josh was pulling me up the steps, and I was sort of laughing, since for the first time it *was* sort of fun. Flashbulbs were going off everywhere, blinding me, so that all I could see were the steps underneath us as we ran up them. I was totally concentrating on holding up the hem of my dress so I didn't trip on it, and had put all my faith in those fingers wrapped around my other hand. I was completely dependent on Josh to lead the way, since I couldn't see a blessed thing.

So when he suddenly stopped, I thought it was because we were at the school doors. I thought we'd stopped because Josh was opening the doors for me. I know it's stupid, but that's what I thought. I could see the doors. We were standing right in front of them. Below us, on the stairs, the reporters were screaming questions and taking pictures. Some moron was yelling, "Kiss her! Kiss her!" which I don't need to tell you was way embarrassing.

And so I just stood there, like a complete IDIOT, waiting for Josh to open the doors, instead of doing the smart thing, which was open the doors myself and get inside where it was safe, where there weren't any cameras or reporters or people yelling "*Kiss her, Kiss her!*"

And then, I don't know how, the next thing I knew Josh had put his arm around me again, dragged me to him, and smashed his mouth against mine.

I swear, that's exactly what it felt like. He just smashed his mouth up against mine, and all these flashes started going off, but believe me, it wasn't like in those books Tina is always reading, where the boy kisses the girl and she sees like fireworks and stuff behind her eyelids. I really WAS seeing lights go off, but they weren't fireworks, they were flashes from cameras. EVERYONE was taking a picture of Princess Mia getting her first kiss.

I am not even kidding. Like it wasn't bad enough that this was my first kiss.

It was my first kiss and *Teen People* was photographing it.

And another thing about those books Tina reads: In those books, when the girl gets her first kiss, she gets this warm gushy feeling inside. She feels like the guy is drawing her soul up from deep within her. I didn't get that feeling. I didn't get that feeling at all. All I got was embarrassed. It didn't feel especially good, having Josh Richter kiss me. All it felt, really, was strange. It felt strange, having this guy stand there and smash his mouth against mine. And you would think that after I'd spent so much time thinking this guy was the greatest thing on earth I'd have felt SOMETHING when he kissed me.

But all I felt was embarrassed.

And like our car ride to the restaurant, I just kept wishing it would end. All I could think was, When is he going to stop doing this? Am I even doing this right? In the movies they move their heads around a lot. Should I move my head around? What am I going to do if he tries to stick his tongue in there, like I used to see him do to Lana? I can't let *Teen People* take a picture of me with some guy's tongue in my mouth; my dad will kill me.

Then, just when I thought I couldn't stand it another minute, that I was going to DIE of embarrassment right there on the steps of Albert Einstein High School, Josh lifted up his head, waved to the reporters, opened the doors to the school, and pushed me inside.

Where, I swear to God, every single person I knew was standing, looking at us.

I am not kidding. There were Tina and her date from Trinity, Dave, looking at me in a sort of shocked way. There were Lilly and Boris, and for once Boris hadn't tucked in anything that wasn't supposed to be tucked. In fact, he almost looked handsome, in a geeky, musical genius kind of way. And Lilly, in a beautiful white dress with spangles all over it, and white roses in her hair. And there were Shameeka and Ling Su with their dates, and a bunch of other people I probably knew but didn't recognize out of their school uniforms, all looking at me with the same sort of expression Tina was wearing, one of total and complete astonishment.

And there was Mr. G, standing by the ticket booth in front of the doors to the cafeteria, where the dance was being held, looking more astonished than anybody.

Except maybe me. I would have to say, out of everybody there, I was the person in the most shock. I mean, Josh Richter HAD just kissed me. JOSH RICHTER had just KISSED me. Josh Richter had just kissed ME.

Did I mention that he'd kissed me ON THE LIPS?

Oh, and that he did it in front of reporters from *TEEN PEOPLE*?

So I'm standing there, and everybody is looking at me, and I could still hear the reporters yelling outside, and inside the cafeteria I could hear the *thump, thump, thump* of the sound system as it ground out some hip-hop, a tribute to our Latino student population, and these thoughts are moving really sluggishly through my head, these thoughts that are saying:

He set you up.

He only asked you out so he could get his picture in the paper.

He's the one who notified the press that you'd be here tonight.

He probably only broke up with Lana just so he could tell his friends he's dating a girl worth three hundred million dollars. He never even noticed you until your picture was on the cover of the *Post*. Lilly was right: That day in Bigelows, he WAS only suffering from a synaptic breakdown when he smiled at you. He probably thinks his chances of getting into Harvard or whatever are way enhanced by the fact that he's the princess of Genovia's boyfriend.

And like a big idiot, I fell for it.

Great. Just great.

Lilly says I'm not assertive enough. Her parents say

I have a tendency to internalize everything and fear confrontation.

My mom says the same thing. That's why she gave me this book, in the hopes that what I won't tell her, I'll at least get out into the open somehow.

If it hadn't turned out that I'm a princess, maybe I might still be all that stuff. You know, unassertive, fearful of confrontation, an internalizer. I probably wouldn't have done what I did next.

Which was turn to Josh and ask, "Why did you do that?"

He was busy patting himself down, trying to find the dance tickets to hand to the sophomores who were manning the ticket table. "Do what?"

"Kiss me like that, in front of everybody."

He found the tickets in his wallet. "I don't know," he said. "Didn't you hear them? They were yelling at me to kiss you. So I did. Why?"

"Because I didn't appreciate it."

"You didn't appreciate it?" Josh looked confused. "You mean you didn't like it?"

"Yes," I said. "That's exactly what I mean. I didn't like it. I didn't like it at all. Because I know you didn't kiss me because you like me. You just kissed me because I'm the princess of Genovia."

Josh looked at me like he thought I was crazy.

"That's crazy," he said. "I like you. I like you a lot."

I said, "You can't like me a lot. You don't even *know*

me. That's why I thought you asked me out. So you could get to know me better. But you haven't tried to get to know me at all. You just wanted to get your picture on *Extra*."

He laughed at that, but I noticed he didn't look me in the eye when he said, "What do you mean, I don't even know you? Of course I know you."

"No, you don't. Because if you did, you wouldn't have ordered me a steak for dinner."

I heard a murmur go around through all of my friends. I guess they recognized the seriousness of Josh's mistake, even if he didn't. He heard them, too, so when he replied, he was talking to them, too. "So I ordered the girl a steak," he said, with his arms open in a so-sue-me sort of way. "That's a crime? It was *filet mignon*, for God's sake."

Lilly said, in her meanest voice, "She's a vegetarian, you sociopath."

This information didn't seem to bother Josh very much. He just shrugged and went, "Oops, my bad."

Then he turned to me and said, "Ready to slide?"

But I had no intention of sliding with Josh. I had no intention of doing anything with Josh, ever again. I couldn't believe, after what I'd just said to him, he thought I'd still *want* to. The guy really *was* a sociopath. How could I ever have thought he'd seen into my soul? How???

Disgusted, I did the only thing a girl can be

expected to do under those circumstances:

I turned my back on him and walked out.

Only, since of course I couldn't go back outside—not if I didn't want *Teen People* to get a nice close-up of me crying—my only recourse was to walk out into the girls' room.

It finally registered on Josh that I was ditching him. By that time, all of his friends had shown up, and they came tumbling through the doors just as Josh said, sounding totally peeved, "Jesus! It was just a kiss!"

I whirled around. "It wasn't just a kiss," I said. I was getting really mad. "Maybe that's how you wanted it to look, like it was just a kiss. But you and I both know what it really was: A media event. And one that you've been planning since you saw me in the *Post*. Well, thank you, Josh, but I can get my own publicity. I don't need *you*."

Then, after holding out my hand to Lars for my journal, I took it and stalked into the girls' room. Which is where I am now, writing this.

God! Can you BELIEVE that? I mean, I ask you: My first kiss—my first kiss ever—and next week it's going to be in every teen magazine in the country. Probably even some international magazines will pick it up, like *Majesty* magazine, which follows the lives of all the young royals in Great Britain and Monaco. They ran a whole article on the wardrobe of Prince Edward's wife, Sophie, once, rating each one of her outfits on a scale of one to ten. They called it "*Out of the Closet.*" I don't suppose it will be too long before *Majesty* magazine starts following me around, rating my wardrobe—and boyfriends—too. I wonder what the caption under the picture of me and Josh will be. "*Young Royal in Love*"?

Excuse me, but *ew.*

And the kicker of it all is that I am totally NOT in love with Josh Richter. I mean, it would have been nice—Who am I kidding? It would have been GREAT—to have a boyfriend. Sometimes I think there really is something wrong with me, that I don't have one.

But the thing is, I would rather not have a boyfriend at all than have one who is only using me for my money or the fact that my father is a prince or for any reason, really, except that he likes me for *me*, and nothing else.

Of course, now that everyone knows I'm a princess, it's going to be kind of hard to tell which guys like me for me and which guys like me for my tiara. But at least I realized the truth about Josh before things went on too long.

How could I have ever liked him? He's such a user. He totally used me! He purposefully hurt Lana and then tried to use me. And I played right into his hands like the stupid sap that I am.

What am I going to do? When my dad sees that photograph, he is going to FLIP OUT. There is no way I will ever be able to explain that it wasn't my fault.

Maybe if I'd punched Josh in the stomach in front of all those cameras, maybe then my dad would believe I was an innocent bystander. . . .

But probably not.

I will never be allowed out of the house with a boy again, ever, for the rest of my natural life.

Uh-oh. I see shoes outside my stall. Somebody is talking to me.

It's Tina. Tina wants to know if I'm all right. Somebody is with her.

Oh my God, I recognize those feet! It's Lilly! Lilly and Tina both want to know if I'm all right!

Lilly is actually speaking to me again. Not criticizing me or complaining about my behavior. She is actually speaking to me in a friendly manner. She's saying through the stall door that she's sorry for laughing at my hair and that she knows she's controlling and that she suffers from a borderline authoritarian personality disorder, and she says she's going to make a concerted effort to stop telling everyone, especially me, what to do.

Wow! Lilly is admitting she did something wrong! I can't believe it! I CAN'T BELIEVE IT!

She and Tina want me to come out and hang out with them. But I told them I don't want to. It would be too awkward, all of them with dates and me by myself like a big dope.

And then Lilly goes, "Oh, that's okay. Michael's

here. He's been hanging around by himself like a big dope all night."

Michael Moscovitz came to a school event??? I can't believe it!! He never goes anywhere, except to like lectures in quantum physics and stuff!!

I have got to see this for myself. I am going out there right now.

More later.

I just woke up from the strangest dream.

In my dream, Lilly and I weren't fighting anymore; she and Tina had become friends; Boris Pelkowski actually turned out to be not so bad when you got him away from his violin; Mr. Gianini said he was raising my nine week grade from an F to a D; I slow-danced with Michael Moscovitz; and Iran bombed Afghanistan, so there wasn't a single picture of me and Josh kissing in any newspaper on the newsstand, since all the papers were filled with photos of war carnage.

But it wasn't a dream. It wasn't a dream at all, none of it! It had all really happened!

Because I woke up this morning with something wet on my face, and when I opened my eyes, I saw that I was lying in the spare bed in Lilly's room, and her brother's sheltie was licking me all over my face. I mean it. I have dog spit all over me.

And I don't even care! Pavlov can drool all over me if he wants to! I have my best friend back! I'm not going to flunk out of ninth grade! My dad isn't going to kill me for kissing Josh Richter!

Oh, and I think Michael Moscovitz might like me!

I can hardly write for happiness.

Little did I know when I came out of the girls' room last night with Lilly and Tina that all this happiness lay in store for me. I was morbidly depressed—yes, *mor-*

bidly. Isn't that a good word? I learned it from Lilly—over what had happened with Josh.

But when I came out of the girls' room, Josh was gone. Lilly told me later that after I publicly humiliated him and then went storming off into the bathroom, Josh went on into the dance, not looking as if he cared too much. Lilly isn't sure what happened after that, because Mr. G asked her and Tina to go and check on me (wasn't that sweet of him?), but I have a feeling Lars might have used one of his special nerve-paralyzing holds on Josh, because the next time I saw him, Josh was slumped over at the Pacific Islander display table with his forehead resting on a model of Krakatoa. He didn't move all night, either, but I just thought that was because of all the champagne he'd had to drink.

Anyway, Lilly and Tina and I joined Boris and Dave—who is really nice, even if he does go to Trinity—and Shameeka and her boyfriend, Allan, and Ling Su and her date, Clifford, at this table they had snagged. It was the Pakistani table, with a display sponsored by the Economics Club, detailing how the market for maunds (a Pakistani unit of measurement) of rice was falling. We moved some of the maunds and sat there anyway, right on the tabletop, so we could see everything.

And then Michael suddenly appeared out of nowhere, looking crescent fresh—isn't that a funny expression? I learned it from Michael—in the tux his mom made him get for his cousin Steve's bar mitzvah.

Michael really didn't have anyone else to hang out with, since Principal Gupta ruled that the Internet is not a culture and therefore cannot have its own table, and so the Computer Club boycotted the Cultural Diversity Dance on principle.

But Michael didn't seem to care what the Computer Club thought, and he's the treasurer! He sat down next to me and asked if I was all right, and then we had fun for a while cracking jokes about how all the cheerleaders sure don't practice any cultural diversity, since they were all dressed in practically the same gown, a slinky black number by Donna Karan. Then somebody started talking about *Star Trek: Deep Space Nine* and whether or not there's caffeine in replicator coffee, and Michael insisted that the matter used to make the things that come out of the replicator is from refuse, which means maybe when you order an ice cream sundae it might be made out of urine, but with the germs and impurities extracted. And we were all getting kind of grossed out when the music changed, and a slow song came on, and everybody left the table to go and dance.

Except for me and Michael, of course. We just sat there amid the maunds of rice.

Which wasn't too bad, actually, since Michael and I never run out of things to talk about—unlike me and Josh. We kept on arguing about the replicator, and then we moved on to who was the more effective leader,

Captain Kirk or Captain Picard, when Mr. Gianini came over and asked me if I was okay.

I said of course, and that was when Mr. G told me he was glad to hear it, and, by the way, based on my latest scores on the practice sheets he'd been giving me every day, I had brought my F in Algebra up to a D, for which he congratulated me, and he urged me to keep up the hard work.

But I credited my improved math performance to Michael, who taught me to stop writing my Algebra notes in my journal, not be so messy with my columns, and to cross things out when I borrow during subtraction. Michael got all embarrassed and claimed not to have had anything to do with it, but Mr. G didn't hear him since he had to hurry off and dissuade a group of Goths from embarking upon a demonstration over the unfair exclusion of a table dedicated to Satan worshipers by the event organizers.

Then a fast song came on and everybody came back, and we sat around and talked about Lilly's show, which Tina Hakim Baba is now going to be producer of, since we found out she gets $50 a week in allowance (she is going to start borrowing teen romances from the library instead of buying them new so that she can use all of her funds for promoting *Lilly Tells It Like It Is*). Lilly asked if I'd mind being the topic for next week's show, titled "The New Monarchy: Royals Who Make a Difference." I gave her exclusive rights to my first public interview if she'd promise to ask me about my feelings on the meat industry.

Then another slow song came on, and everybody went to go and dance to it. Michael and I were left sitting amid the rice again, and I was about to ask him who he'd choose to spend eternity with if nuclear Armageddon wiped out the rest of the population, Buffy the Vampire Slayer or Sabrina the Teenage Witch, when he asked me if I wanted to dance!

I was so surprised, I said sure without even thinking about it. And then the next thing I knew, I was dancing my first dance with a boy who wasn't my dad!

And it was a *slow* one!

Slow dancing is *strange*. It isn't even dancing, really. It's more like standing there with your arms around the other person, moving from one foot to the other in time to the music. And I guess you aren't supposed to talk—at least, nobody else around us was talking. I guess I could sort of see why, since you're so busy *feeling* stuff it's hard to think of anything to say. I mean, Michael *smelled* so good—like Ivory soap—and *felt* so good—the dress Grandmère picked out for me was pretty and everything, but I was kind of cold in it, so it was nice to stand close to Michael, who was so warm—that it was next to impossible to *say* anything.

I guess Michael felt the same way, because even though when we were sitting there on the table with all the rice neither of us ever shut up, we had so much to talk about, when we were dancing together neither of us said a word.

But the minute the song was over Michael started talking again, asking me if I wanted some Thai iced tea from the Thai Culture table, or maybe some edamame from the Japanese Anime Club's table. For somebody who'd never been to a single school event—aside from Computer Club meetings—Michael sure was making up for lost time in his enthusiasm over being at this one.

And that was how the rest of the night went: We sat around and talked during the fast songs and danced during the slow ones.

And you know, to tell the truth, I couldn't say which I liked better, talking to Michael or dancing with him. They were both so . . . interesting.

In different ways, of course.

When the dance was over we all piled into the limo Mr. Hakim Baba sent to pick up Tina and Dave (the news vans had all left by then, since the story about the bombing had broken; I suppose they went to go stake out the Iranian embassy). I called my mom on the limo cell phone and told her where I was and asked if I could spend the night at Lilly's, since that's where we were all headed. She said yes without asking any questions, which led me to believe that she'd already talked to Mr. G and that he'd filled her in on the night's events. I wonder if he told her he'd raised my F to a D.

You know, he could have given me a D plus. I have been nothing but supportive of his relationship with my mother. That kind of loyalty ought to be rewarded.

Dr. and Dr. Moscovitz seemed kind of surprised when all ten of us—twelve, if you count Lars and Wahim—showed up at their door. They were especially surprised to see Michael; they hadn't realized he'd left his room. But they let us take over the living room, where we played End of the World until Lilly's and Michael's dad finally came out in his pajamas and said everybody had to go home, he had an early appointment with his tai chi instructor.

Everybody said good-bye and piled into the elevator, except for me and the Moscovitzes. Even Lars hitched a ride back to the Plaza—once I had been locked down for the night, his responsibilities were over. I made him promise not to tell my dad about the kiss. He said he wouldn't, but you can never tell with guys; they have this weird code of their own, you know? I was reminded of it when I saw Lars and Michael giving each other high fives right before he left.

The strangest thing out of everything that happened last night is that I found out what Michael does in his room all the time. He showed me, but he made me swear never to tell anyone, including Lilly. I probably shouldn't even write it down here, in case someone ever finds this book and reads it. All I can say is Lilly's been wasting her time worshiping Boris Pelkowski; there's a musical genius in her very own family.

And to think, he's never had one lesson! He taught himself how to play the guitar—and he writes all his own songs! The one he played for me is called "Tall Drink of Water." It's about this very tall pretty girl who doesn't know this boy is in love with her. I predict that one day it will be number one on the *Billboard* chart. Michael Moscovitz could one day be as famous as Puff Daddy.

It wasn't until everyone was gone that I realized how tired I was. It had been a really long day. I had broken up with a boy I had only been out on half a date with. That can be very emotionally wearing.

Still, I woke up way early, like I always do when I spend the night at Lilly's. I lay there with Pavlov in my arms and listened to the sound of the morning traffic on Fifth Avenue, which isn't really very loud, since the Moscovitzes had their windows soundproofed. As I lay there, I thought, Really, I am a very lucky girl. Things had looked pretty bad there for a while. But isn't it funny how everything kind of works itself out in the end?

I hear stirrings in the kitchen. Maya must be there, pouring out glasses of pulpless orange juice for breakfast. I'm going to go see if she needs any help.

I don't know why, but I AM SO HAPPY!

I guess it doesn't take much, does it?

Sunday Night

Grandmère showed up at the loft today with Dad in tow. Dad wanted to find out how things went at the dance. Lars didn't tell him! God, I *love* my bodyguard. And Grandmère wanted to let me know that she has to go away for a week, so our princess lessons are suspended for the time being. She says it's time to pay her yearly visit to somebody named Baden-Baden. I suppose he's friends with that other guy she used to hang around with, Boutros-Boutros Something-or-other.

Even *my grandmother* has a boyfriend.

Anyway, she and Dad just showed up out of the blue, and you should have seen my mom's face. She looked about ready to heave. Especially when Grandmère started bossing her around about how messy the loft is (I've been too busy lately to clean).

To distract Grandmère from my mom, I told her I'd walk her back to her limo, and on the way I told her all about Josh, and she was way interested, since the story had everything in it that she likes, reporters and cute boys and people getting their hearts totally stomped on and stuff like that.

Anyway, while we were standing on the corner saying good-bye until next week (*YES!* No princess lessons for a whole week! She shoots; she scores!) the Blind Guy walked by, tapping his cane. He stopped at the corner and stood there, waiting for his next victim to come along and help him cross the street. Grandmère saw this and totally fell for it. She was like, "Amelia, go and help that poor young man."

But, of course, I knew better. I said, "No way."

"Amelia!" Grandmère was shocked. "One of the most important traits in a princess is her unfailing kindess to strangers. Now, go and help that young man cross the street."

I said, "No way, Grandmère. If you think he needs help so much, *you* do it."

So Grandmère, all bent out of shape—and I guess intent on showing me how unfailingly kind she is—went up to the Blind Guy and said in this fakey voice, "Let me help you, young man. . . ."

The Blind Guy grabbed Grandmère by the arm. I guess he liked what he felt, because the next thing I knew, he was going, "Oh, thank you so much, ma'am," and he and Grandmère were crossing Spring Street.

I didn't think the Blind Guy was going to try to feel up my grandmother. I really didn't, or I wouldn't have let her help him. I mean, Grandmère is no spring chicken, if you know what I mean. I couldn't imagine any guy, even a blind one, feeling her up.

But next thing I knew, Grandmère was yelling her head off, and both her driver and our neighbor who used to be a man came running out to help her.

But Grandmère didn't need any help. She whacked the Blind Guy across the face with her purse so hard his sunglasses went flying off. After that there was no doubt about it: The Blind Guy can see.

And let me tell you something: I don't think he'll be taking any more trips down our street for a while.

After all that yelling, it was almost a blessing to go inside and work on my Algebra homework for the rest of the day. I needed some peace and quiet.

Keep reading! There's more!

Check out the following pages
for more about Mia's further adventures,
as well as information on other books by Meg Cabot.

- Read an excerpt from the second Princess Diaries book, *Princess in the Spotlight*.

- Find out more about the rest of the Princess Diaries series (If you thought Mia had a hard time with Algebra, just wait till she gets to Geometry!).

- Read up on Meg's other cool characters, like a girl who sees ghosts, and one who saves the president's life.

- Read an exclusive interview with Meg!

- Info about Meg's ultra-fabulous website—the one spot to find out about new books and what Meg's up to, and to read her online diary.

- And much more!

From

THE PRINCESS DIARIES, VOLUME II

Princess
IN THE
SPOTLIGHT

Sunday, October 26, 2 a.m., Lilly's bedroom

Okay, I just have one question: Why does it always have to go from bad to worse for me?

I mean, apparently it is not enough that

1. I was born lacking any sort of mammary growth gland
2. My feet are as long as a normal person's thigh
3. I'm the sole heir to the throne of a European principality
4. My grade point average is still slipping in spite of everything
5. I have a secret admirer who will not declare himself, and all of America is going to know it after Monday night's broadcast of my exclusive interview on *Twenty-Four/Seven*

No, in addition to all of that, I happen to be the only one of my friends who still has yet to be French-kissed.

Seriously. For next week's show, Lilly insisted on shooting what she calls a Scorsesian confessional, in which she hopes to illustrate the degenerate lows to which today's youth have sunk. So she made us all confess to the camera our worst sins, and it turns out Shameeka, Tina Hakim Baba, Ling Su, and Lilly have ALL had boys' tongues in their mouths. *All of them.*

Except for me.

God, I am such a reject. The only boy who has ever kissed me did it just so he could get his picture in the paper.

Yeah, there was some tongue action, but believe me, I kept my lips way closed.

And since I have never been French-kissed, and had nothing good to confess on the show, Lilly decided to punish me by giving me a Dare. She didn't even ask me if I would prefer a Truth.

Lilly dared me I wouldn't drop an eggplant onto the sidewalk from her sixteenth-story bedroom window.

I said I most certainly would, even though of course, I totally didn't want to. I mean, how stupid. Somebody could seriously get hurt. I am all for illustrating the degenerate lows to which America's teens have sunk, but I wouldn't want anybody to get their head bashed in.

But what could I do? It was a Dare. I had to go along with it. I mean, it's bad enough I've never been Frenched. I don't want to be branded a wimp, too.

And I couldn't exactly stand there and go, well, all

right, I may never have been French-kissed by a boy, but I have been the recipient of a love letter that was written by one. A boy, I mean.

I guess the knowledge that somewhere in the world there is a boy who likes me gave me a sense of empowerment—something I certainly could have used during my interview with Beverly Bellerieve, but whatever. I may not be able to form a coherent sentence when there is a television camera aimed in my direction, but I am at least capable, I decided, of throwing an eggplant out the window.

Lilly was shocked. I had never accepted a Dare like that before.

I can't really explain why I did it. Maybe I was just trying to live up to my new reputation as a very Josie-ish type of girl.

Or maybe I was more scared of what Lilly would try to make me do if I said no. Once she made me run up and down the hallway naked. Not the hallway in the Moscovitzes' apartment, either. The hallway *outside* of it.

Whatever my reasons, I soon found myself sneaking past the Drs. Moscovitz—who were lounging around in sweatpants in the living room, with stacks of important medical journals all around their chairs—though Lilly's father was reading a copy of *Sports Illustrated* and Lilly's mom was reading *Cosmo*—and creeping into the kitchen.

I found an eggplant in the vegetable crisper. I hid it under my shirt so the Drs. Moscovitz wouldn't see me sneaking back into their daughter's room holding a giant ovoid fruit, something sure to cause unwanted questions.

Then, while Lilly narrated gravely into the microphone about how Mia Thermopolis was about to strike a blow for good girls everywhere, and Shameeka filmed, I opened the window, made sure no innocent bystanders were below, and then. . . .

"Bomb's away," I said, like in the movies.

It *was* kind of cool seeing this huge purple eggplant—it was the size of a football—tumbling over and over in the air as it fell. There are enough streetlamps on Fifth Avenue, where the Moscovitzes live, for us to see it as it plummeted downward, even though it was night. Down and down the eggplant went, past the windows of all the psychoanalysts and investment bankers (the only people who can afford apartments in Lilly's building) until suddenly—

SPLAT!

The eggplant hit the sidewalk.

Only it didn't just hit the sidewalk. It *exploded* on the sidewalk, sending bits of eggplant flying everywhere—mostly all over an M1 city bus that was driving by at the time, but quite a lot all over a Jaguar that had been idling nearby.

While I was leaning out the window, admiring the

splatter pattern the eggplant's pulp had made all over the street and sidewalk, the driver-side door of the Jaguar opened up, and a man got out from behind the wheel, just as the doorman to Lilly's building stepped out from beneath the awning over the front doors, and looked up—

Suddenly, someone threw an arm around my waist and yanked me backward, right off my feet.

"Get down!" Michael hissed, pulling me down to the parquet.

We all ducked. Well, Lilly, Michael, Shameeka, Ling Su, and Tina ducked. I was already on the floor.

Where had Michael come from? I hadn't even known he was home—and I'd asked, believe me, on account of the whole running-down-the-hallway-naked thing. Just in case, and all.

But Lilly had said he was at a lecture on quasars over at Columbia and wouldn't be home for hours.

"Are you guys stupid, or what?" Michael wanted to know. "Don't you know, besides the fact that it's a good way to kill someone, it's also against the law to drop things out a window in New York City?"

"Oh, Michael," Lilly said, disgustedly. "Grow up. It was just a common garden vegetable."

"I'm serious." Michael looked mad. "If anyone saw Mia do that just now, she could be arrested."

"No, she couldn't," Lilly said. "She's a minor."

"She could still go to juvenile court. You'd better

not be planning on airing that footage on your show," Michael said.

Oh, my God, Michael was defending my honor! Or at least trying to make sure I didn't end up in juvenile court. It was just so sweet.

Lilly went, "I most certainly am."

"Well, you'd better edit out the parts that show Mia's face."

Lilly stuck her chin out. "No way."

"Lilly, everybody knows who Mia is. If you air that segment, it will be all over the news that the princess of Genovia was caught on tape dropping projectiles out the window of her friend's high-rise apartment. Get a clue, will you?"

Michael had let go of my waist, I noticed, with regret.

"Lilly, Michael's right," Tina Hakim Baba said. "We better edit that part out. Mia doesn't need any more publicity than she has already."

And Tina didn't even *know* about the *TwentyFour/ Seven* thing.

Lilly got up and stomped back toward the window. She started to lean out—checking, I guess, to see whether the doorman and the owner of the Jaguar were still there—but Michael jerked her back.

"Rule Number One," he said. "If you insist on dropping something out the window, never, ever check to see if anybody is standing down there, looking up.

They will see you look out and figure out what apartment you are in. Then you will be blamed for dropping whatever it was. Because no one but the guilty party would be looking out the window under such circumstances."

"Wow, Michael," Shameeka said admiringly. "You sound like you've done this before."

Not only that. He sounded like Dirty Harry.

Which was just how I felt when I dropped that eggplant out the window. Like Dirty Harry.

And it had felt good—but not quite so good as having Michael rush to my defense like that.

Michael said, "Let's just say I used to have a very keen interest in experimenting with the earth's gravitational pull."

Wow. There is so much I don't know about Lilly's brother. Like he used to be a juvenile delinquent!

Could a computer-genius-slash-juvenile-delinquent ever be interested in a flat-chested princess like myself? He did save my life tonight (well, okay: he saved me from possible community service).

It's not a French kiss, or a slow dance, or even an admission he's the author of that anonymous letter.

But it's a start.

READ ALL THE BOOKS ABOUT MIA:

The Princess Diaries

Mia Thermopolis is pretty sure there's nothing worse than being a five-foot-nine, flat-chested freshman, who also happens to be flunking Algebra. Is she ever in for a surprise! First her mom announces that she's dating Mia's Algebra teacher. Then her dad has to go and reveal that he's the crown prince of Genovia. And guess who still doesn't have a date for the Cultural Diversity Dance?

The Princess Diaries, Volume II:
Princess in the Spotlight

Just when Mia thought she had the whole princess thing under control, things get out of hand, fast. In just one national prime-time interview, Mia manages to enrage her best friend, practically get one of her teachers fired, and alienate all of Genovia. Add an announcement from her mother and letters from a secret admirer, and Mia's swept up in more royal intrigue than even she could have thought possible.

The Princess Diaries, Volume III:
Princess in Love

While Mia may seem like the luckiest girl ever, the truth is, she spends all her time doing one of three things: preparing for her nerve-racking entrée into Genovian society, slogging through the congestion unique to Manhattan in December, and avoiding further smooches from her boyfriend, Kenny. Being a princess in love is not the fairy tale it's supposed to be . . . or is it?

The Princess Diaries, Volume IV:
Princess in Waiting

On her first official visit to Genovia, Mia is having a rough time. While her fashion sense is applauded, her installation of parking meters has been met with criticism. Add that to her princess lessons with Grandmère, her inability to quit biting her nails, and her canceled dates with the boy of her dreams, and Mia is beginning to wonder if there's anything she *can* do—besides inheriting an unwanted royal title, of course.

The Princess Diaries, Volume IV and a Half:

Project Princess

It's spring break, and Mia can think of a few good ways to spend her well-earned vacation from princess lessons and, of course, Algebra. And what better way to divide her time than between building houses for underprivileged families and kissing her boyfriend, Michael?

The Princess Diaries, Volume V:

Princess in Pink

Things are looking up for Mia: She's the newest staffer on the school paper, she's about to get a new sister or brother, and her completion of freshman Algebra is right around the corner. Best of all, the prom is only weeks away. But with Michael unenthusiastic about spending the night in a tux, and a workers' strike threatening the very existence of the big night, will Mia ever get to wear her beautiful pink prom dress?

The Princess Diaries, Volume VI:
Princess in Training

Even though Grandmère thinks that being student body president is good practice for ruling a small country, Mia is less than thrilled when Lilly nominates her as a candidate. After all, isn't sophomore Geometry enough for one girl to tackle? And with Michael at college, Mia is working hard to think of any reason to go to high school at all. Is this princess in training up for the challenge of sophomore year?

The Princess Present:
A PRINCESS DIARIES BOOK (VOLUME VI AND A HALF)

It's off to Genovia for the holidays, but despite the vacation, Mia has plenty on her mind. Mostly, she's worried about her present for Michael. But she's about to learn that what makes a perfect present has nothing to do with international express couriers—and everything to do with love. Though some shiny ribbon never hurts, either.

Available April 2006!

The Princess Diaries, Volume VII:

Party Princess

It's the spring of Mia's sophomore year, and she's smack in the middle of a musical moneymaking scheme to save the student government. After all, if she can't balance the student budget, what chance does she have of running a country one day? On top of all this, Michael tells her she's not a "party girl." Whatever that means!

Available June 2006!

Sweet Sixteen Princess:
A PRINCESS DIARIES BOOK (VOLUME VII AND A HALF)

Spring is here—and so is Mia's sixteenth birthday. Sweet sixteen, at last! Will Mia be able to find self-actualization? Find out if Mia's big day is a raging success or a royal failure.

ILLUSTRATED BY
CHESLEY McLAREN

Princess Lessons

Etiquette, comportment and, of course, dating!
Everything you need to know about being a true
princess, with advice from Grandmère, Paolo,
Mia's friends and, of course, Mia herself!

Perfect Princess

Big and small, old and new, real and imaginary—
all kinds of princesses exhibit perfection in their
own way. Don't delay: Find out who made this
royal roster rule, and begin your own reign!

Holiday Princess

A princess always knows how to celebrate the
holidays. There's Christmas, Hanukkah, Yule,
Chinese New Year . . . you get the hint. How will
you celebrate this holiday season? From gift giving
to what to eat, Mia and her friends have a few ideas
to make your holidays perfect.

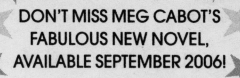

How to Be Popular

Do you want to be popular?

Everyone wants to be popular—or at least, Stephanie Landry does. Steph's been the least popular girl in her class since a certain cherry Super Big Gulp catastrophe five years earlier.

Does being popular matter?

It matters very much—to Steph. That's why this year, she has a plan to get in with the It Crowd in no time flat. She's got a secret weapon: An old book called—what else?—*How to Be Popular*.

What does it take to be popular?

All Steph has to do is follow the instructions in The Book, and soon she'll be partying with the It Crowd (including school quarterback Mark Finley) instead of sitting on The Hill Saturday nights, stargazing with her nerdy best pal Becca, and even nerdier Jason (now kind of hot, but still), whose passion for astronomy Steph once shared.

Who needs red dwarves when you're invited to the hottest parties in town?

But don't forget the most important thing about popularity!

It's easy to become popular. What isn't so easy? Staying that way.

★ ALL-*American* GIRL ★

What if you were going about your ordinary life when, all of a sudden, you accidentally saved the president's life? This is just what happened to ordinary high school sophomore Samantha Madison. Now everyone in the country thinks she's a hero. But the number-one reason Samantha's life has just gone completely insane is that the president's son might just be in love with her. Gulp!

Ready OR *Not*

Samantha Madison's parents think she's ready to learn the value of a dollar. Her art teacher thinks she's ready for "life drawing" (which means "naked people"!!). And her boyfriend (who happens to be the president's son) seems to think she's ready to take their relationship to the Next Level. Everyone thinks Samantha is ready. Everyone except Samantha.

TEEN IDOL

Jenny Greenley is so good at keeping secrets that she's her school newspaper's anonymous advice columnist. And when hotter-than-hot Hollywood star Luke Striker comes to her small town, she's the one in charge of keeping his identity under wraps. But it's not easy. And soon everyone—the paparazzi, the town, and the tabloids—is dragging this small-town girl into the public spotlight.

 AVALON HIGH

Avalon High seems like a typical high school, attended by typical students: There's Lance, the jock. Jennifer, the cheerleader. And Will, senior class president, quarterback, and all-around good guy.

But not everybody at Avalon High is who they appear to be . . . not even, as new student Ellie is about to discover, herself. What part does she play in the drama that is unfolding? What if the bizarre chain of events and coincidences she has pieced together means—like the court of King Arthur—tragedy is fast approaching Avalon High?

Worst of all, what if there's nothing she can do about it?

the mediator

Mia Thermopolis is a princess, Jenny Greenley is a tabloid target, and Samantha Madison is a national heroine, but Susannah Simon is an altogether different kind of girl. The star of Meg Cabot's Mediator series, Suze can see ghosts. Which is kind of a pain most of the time, but when Suze moves to California and finds Jesse, the ghost of a nineteenth-century hottie haunting her bedroom, things begin to look up.

Finally, don't miss these two
irresistible love stories by Meg Cabot.
All the fun of *The Princess Diaries*,
with a Jane Austen twist!

Nicola *and the* Viscount

It's only her first London Season, but sixteen-year-old
Nicola has made up her mind: Handsome, charming,
poetry-reading Lord Sebastian is, simply, a god. So when
the divine viscount starts paying special attention to her,
Nicola is certain she's found her destiny.

Everything is perfect until the infuriating—and dis-
turbingly handsome—Nathaniel Sheridan begins to cast
doubt on the viscount's character . . . and on Nicola's feelings.

Victoria *and the* Rogue

Wealthy young heiress Lady Victoria Arbuthnot is accus-
tomed to handling her own affairs—and everyone else's. So
when she's suddenly sent to London to find a husband,
Victoria quickly finds a perfect English gentleman.

Everything is just as she wants it—that is, if the raffish
young ship captain Jacob Carstairs would stop meddling in
her plans.

An *Interview...*

Q: First of all, how do you write so many books?

A: My mom made me take typing in high school because she despaired of me ever being able to get any kind of job other than secretarial, due to my total lack of skills at food service. I now type 80 words a minute. I highly recommend Bloomington High School South's Typing I and II to all aspiring authors.

Q: You write books for both teens and adults— what are the differences?

A: In the adult books, I can use bad words and have more explicit sex scenes. Plus, they're longer. That's about the only difference to me. In my YAs, I always have to go back and do a search for all the swear words and take them out before I send them to my publisher.

Q: Do you read books for teens?

A: I absolutely do. I run an online book club for teens (**www.megcabotbookclub.com**) and every month I pick a book for us all to read. We've done books by Susan Juby, Louise Rennison, Maud Hart Lovelace, Mary Stewart, Sonya Sones, and new authors as well, such as Elizabeth Lenhard and Wendy Mass. I have to read a lot of teen books to find appropriate picks for the club. It's not easy—but it's fun!

Q: What are you working on next?

A: I believe there will be something involving teen witches (*Jinx*)—although of course *my* teen witches won't be riding around on brooms or making things appear from nowhere. They're *real* witches. And then there's my first stand-alone featuring a heroine who is actually—gasp—*popular* (tentatively titled *Tommy Sullivan Is a Freak*)—but will she still be popular by the end of the book? Additionally, I'll be working on my books for adults, including a humorous mystery series featuring an amateur sleuth who works in an undergrad dorm at a large New York college (the Heather Wells series) and the first in a series of books featuring a recent college grad who can't seem to keep her mouth shut called *Queen of Babble*. And I might have a few other things up my sleeve!

www.megcabot.com
The ultimate source for all things Meg!

*L*og on to Meg Cabot's very own website and enter the unique world of this fantastic author:

- **Meg's Diary**—her very own blog!

- **Meg's Books**—all about all her books!

- **Meg Cabot Mobile**—get exclusive Meg text messages!

- **About Meg**—everything you ever wanted to know about Meg!

- **Meg's Book Club**—Meg's own book club just for teen girls, where fans can chat with one another, and even with Meg!

A GARRY MARSHALL Film

Disney's

· THE ·

PRINCESS
DIARIES

2-DISC SPECIAL EDITION

· THE ·

PRINCESS
DIARIES · 2
ROYAL ENGAGEMENT

SHE ROCKS. SHE RULES.
SHE REIGNS!

BOTH NOW AVAILABLE
TO OWN ON DVD